Suburban Surreal

A COLLECTION OF DARK TALES

by

Gary J Davison

SUBURBAN SURREAL

August Afternoons

H ot? I couldn't begin to tell you enough about how hot it was; stifling heat. These had to be the hottest August afternoons that Larkswood, and its inhabitants, had seen for all the years this street had stood. The bleaching sunlight had the place buzzing with activity: all kinds of people going about their more than usual business.

A worn old football was kicked and chased along this road by kids with sunburnt arms, to the distant chimes of an ice cream van, now only a street away. While some resident stray dogs buoyantly scampered along with their tongues almost reaching the pavement, as they joined this almost impossible task of cooling down in this withering sun, on a scorching high noon in August.

This strangely compelling scene was viewed with great interest from the front window of flat 21. Kahl stood in this unusually cool room, yet burned like he never had before. Heatstroke, by definition, is hardly the most pleasurable sensation to possess, and Kahl knew that at this moment in time better than most. And there was still so much to do having only moved in two days ago; but what really needed doing was done. Everything else could wait.

Kahl wasn't keen on the choice of wallpaper inherited from the previous occupant, but that could be corrected later; so no great problems there. But the living room, though, maintained an atmosphere within it: a sense of oppression. Did Kahl give this unusual presence a second thought? Not a chance. He was all too aware that everything about him felt oppressed by this emaciating heat. As if the entire planet was reducing into charred and glowing embers.

The bloody noise! Larkswood itself was pleasant enough, and Kahl counted his blessings to have acquired accommodation along this street; but it was not a place to visit if in search of quiet sanctuary. He was pleased the living room owned a colder temperature, so the windows didn't have to be opened. Kahl bent down to lift his potted plant from the floor and placed it onto the white window sill, to give it a degree of attentive heat from the sun. It desperately needed this after those cack-handed removal men nearly destroyed the bloody thing while in transit.

Kahl loved his Weeping Fig, which by now had shed almost half of its leaves. Luckily, with the correct degree of nurturing all could soon be well. A Weeping Fig will bask in the spring, but thrives throughout the summer. And several drops of liquid plant feed would rectify this leafy shrub, hopefully, in just a few short days. Kahl wished his heatstroke could be cured just as easily. With two days spent running errands, back and forth – all of necessity – but how he longed for an ounce of respite from this unforgiving season as he made every effort within him to get his plant healthy once again. By now the fatigue had so weakened him he sank backwards into the comfy cloth embroidered settee that faced the sun flooded window.

Studiously scrutinizing this unpalatable diamond chequered wall covering reminded Kahl of a fancy dress party on the nursery school lawn to celebrate the Queen's Silver Jubilee. One kid, whom he'd never formed any particular acquaintance with, was dressed as a Harlequin clown. A tea party of bunting-strewn tables with orange juice, sausage rolls, roast beef sandwiches, jam sponge cakes, raspberry trifle and all of the union flags a sovereign proud country could fly.

As everyone joined in the party games the Harlequin kid decided he needed the toilet, but the school doors were locked. Unable to rouse any teacher's attention, the kid sneaked away and quietly shit in the sandpit. The stench was intolerable. Young Kahl became sensible to this horrific odour in the summer breeze and vomited violently. The thought of that long distant event rendered Kahl nauseous, even now, to this very day.

The heatstroke had this 25 year old delirious with fever; and the sunlight through the brown wooden framed window was now at its most intense. Sunk back in his seat, Kahl squinted at the wallpaper through his increasingly distorted vision. As he studied the pattern of the diamond chequered covering, a brief movement from inside this paper caught his eye. Kahl rubbed his tired eyes and wiped the fevered perspiration from his brow, and looked again. As he watched, a forming shape of some kind became increasingly apparent.

Kahl stared in disbelief, becoming horribly aware of an unconquerable paralysis of his body. Only able to recognise this apparition inside the wallpaper as a Harlequin clown of some type; being a thing of no real discernible feature. To Kahl's terror, it sprang with an elegant leap from the wall, as if finally freed from its shackles.

This shape now stood free from the wall as Kahl's bloodshot eyes froze, while his body could make no movement of its own volition. For all that this clown stood alone, independently, it now had such a definitive shape about it, but no definite outline: as if it's being was somehow incomplete.

A blood red mask with the tiniest eyeholes guarded the secrets behind this shape. With a deathly pale head, free of any feature other than a circular lipless orifice and drooling yellow gum. The satin-like loose-fitting chequered garment of red, blue and green, on closer inspection, was more of an actual skin. It must have been, as Kahl had never encountered any fabric like it. And it's nimble guile facilitated by soft white plimsolls. Though again to Kahl, the shoes were more of this thing's own physical form than anything worn about it.

In his reclined paralysis, Kahl struggled within himself to overcome this mirage of his mind that loomed before him. For all he could hear the playful shrieks and echoes of a bouncing ball in the sunshine, this experience was the polar opposite of any ambient dog-day. Within the blink of an eye the clown leapt again, springing directly in front of Kahl: introducing itself only with the most elegant curtsy. With the high noon sun making only a silhouette of the form, it suddenly dropped into a squat position, resting its elbows on its thighs.

If this was all a dream, Kahl wanted to wake up now more than ever and struggled in himself to do so. Suddenly he began to hear a whisper of a breath that could only be emanating from the clown: a series of short, erratic breaths. All too soon Kahl was revived by an old but foul familiar smell. Now focused and to his horror, he realised what the exertions of the creature had produced. A pile of semi-digested roast beef and trifle lay directly beneath it; the loosest discharge seeping into the cracks of the laminate wood flooring.

The clown sprang erect in shadow to graciously blow a condescending kiss, and took one step backwards to take a bow. This overbearing stench caused Kahl to violently vomit several jets of luminous bile into his own lap. He closed his eyes to regain his composure for a moment or two; on opening them again, the clown and its discharge had vanished. The young man lay there exhausted, hopelessly attempting to come to terms with this fever-induced ordeal.

That night Kahl was plagued by a restless agitation, with terror and danger dominating his dreams. He bore the fatigue of the previous afternoon; psychologically weakened as well as physically. But soon, the sun was strong, though it sat slightly lower in the sky at this time of morning.

Kahl watched again from his window to see the street about him slowly populate just as it had the day before. The Weeping Fig was fed with every effort and strength he could muster, in a hope to soon have the plant restored to its usual dark and glossy foliage. As he inspected the smooth grey bark of the trunk, he noticed many tiny pink dots strewn about it. Convinced of an infestation by some creepy spider mites and their eggs, he dropped in a touch more liquid feed for good measure. Now satisfied, Kahl slumped back into his seat again as the sun began a climb to its zenith.

A sudden shock jolted Kahl from his day-dream like malaise. A football had struck the window. It was again high noon as he wiped away the beads of sweat from his fevered brow with an unusually heavy arm. His eyes cautiously glanced left: to the area of the wall that to his own senses, had come alive. There was movement again from inside this chequered covering, as Kahl now found himself in the stages of paralysis that had tormented him the afternoon before. The clown leapt from the wall without warning; while Kahl's desperate attempts of crying out for help failed him.

The clown gracefully pirouetted across the floor; coming to an abrupt halt with a gracious curtsy between the illuminated high noon window and Kahl himself. It once again rendered in silhouette to the same squatted position, as Kahl closed his eyes on hearing the clown's short and erratic breaths begin the forced evacuation. This provocative act induced Kahl's violent vomiting as the clown took one step back while blowing a kiss of contempt. As the nausea subsided, Kahl opened his eyes; once again he found himself alone. An ice cream van roused him to reality with its loud chimes as a queue formed alongside it for a cooling ice lolly on this blazing August afternoon.

The night lasted too long. In bed, suspicious of the faintest sound, Kahl sat propped up on a pile of old flat pillows, in dread of an appearance by the being that disturbed his every thought and action. The air was cool. Every glint in the night sky was visible from a curtain-less window. A shooting star arched its way across space, leaving in its wake a fantastical trail of stardust. Such a sight would usually beguile Kahl, but tonight, he didn't care. His heatstroke bound him in torment. Yet the fever waned somewhat as Kahl vowed to repel any further paralysis wickedly bestowed by his silent dancing master, dare it manifest again. Just as the late night once more transformed into an early day, Kahl finally fell into a short, restless sleep.

Unbroken sunbeams flooded this street with summer once more. Though it was early, Larkswood didn't possess the previous morning's hectic activity. Kahl relished this tranquil moment while browsing over the small, oval waxy leaves and drooping slender branches of his Weeping Fig. These soothing seconds were not to last too long, as the spider mites had now infested the entire plant. On Kahl reaching for a magnifying glass from a wall mounted shelf, he closely inspected the ailing shrub. To his absolute horror there were no mites, only hundreds of tiny perforations covering the plant as pores cover the human skin.

Following several droplets of feed, this keen scrutiny uncovered two new shoots protruding from the base of the trunk. They bore a much paler hue about them, and had sprouted tiny talons at their tips; as opposed to a bud of some sort. Something was very wrong with this plant, which was by no means thriving; on the contrary it now looked worse than ever before. The plant feed directions label had been studiously double checked more than once, so why did the plant appear to be rejecting this remedy? With the street remaining desolate and the fever less empowering, Kahl left the Fig by the window and decided upon a short walk to clear his head. It was an idea that a brief encounter with the outside world might put these strange events into a more understandable and manageable perspective.

Again it was now high noon as Kahl assumed a reclined position and waited for this unwelcomed guest to manifest once more. His resolve had never been greater as the sun's ascent finally reached its unforgiving peak. He began to feign fever only seconds before the Harlequin's leaping form sprang from within the confines of the wall. It seamlessly glided across the floor as though performing a tightrope act, before allowing one final gracious curtsy. Again it confronted Kahl in silhouette as a blistering sun shined on naively. The usual paralysis was resisted from every fibre within: astonishingly, it worked.

As the clown settled into a squatted position, Kahl heard an urgent and violent rustling sound. The Harlequin flinched in surprise; turning with an unnerving speed. The Weeping Fig was quivering furiously from side to side; now just as alive as the monstrosity opposite.

The clown lunged towards the plant as its two freshly sprouted shoots sprang uncoiling from the Fig, directly into the eye holes of the creature's mask. Just as quickly the shoots recoiled again, with the talons gripping not only the mask, but two purple eyeballs: each adorned with ribbon like severed muscles and still pulsating nerves.

The creature covered its spewing eye sockets with crossed arms as it squealed, and collapsed to the floor: its form contorting in spasms of agony.

With an unhinged determination about him, and bent on revenge, Kahl quickly reached to his small mahogany table, grabbing for his sturdy, blunted letter opener.

Springing from his seat, he forcefully plunged the blade to awkwardly rip the length of the clown's stomach. Where mucus glazed black and blue entrails spilled out across the floor so capaciously, that any great beast could happily wallow in these bowels.

Kahl violently vomited at the sight and stench that lay before him. He wiped his eyes with a handkerchief taken from his pocket. No carnage; not one remnant of the last horrific few moments remained. His Weeping Fig was healthy once again...

This traumatised man sat for several silent hours that seemed like several silent days. Over and over in his own mind he speculated on his frail condition of sanity. He was surely sensible, but sensible only to this: the echoes of the clown's hideous screams would never be forgotten, and will haunt every August afternoon in flat 21 at Larkswood, forever.

Maddie's Doll

This hollowed old pumpkin scrapes along the pavement, revealing the signs of wear and tear about its scary face; with the coarse string attached tailored for carrying rather than dragging. And although it's now November 5th and the withered leaves scatter the ground, the air is surprisingly mild, and far from being the coldest day of 1986. But for Maddie, this weather chills her little bare feet, as she stamps them down on the paving stones in her familiar efforts to keep them warmed while dragging this new toy along. And wearing her favourite flower patterned dress all fraying at the hem, she lifts away the dirty hair that's stuck to her face with those tiny fingers.

With the pumpkin suddenly fragmenting, four year old Maddie Josey discards it on arriving back at her Nana's house on Halstead Hill. With her nose running like two little waxy taps, she lifts up high on her tiptoes and pulls on the stiff handle of the back door. She whimpers to discover it's locked, but because her cries are too often ignored, Maddie wipes a straying tear from her dirty, round cheeked face. This recurring situation isn't such a shock to the system of this infant as it could have been; as every day appears identical in her vacuous young life – too bleak with disappointment and so barren the outlook.

Appearing from behind a drape curtained window of the adjoining residence are the concerned features of this notoriously nosey neighbour, the stout and grey haired Kitty Stiff. For the past several months she's found herself increasingly concerned for the wellbeing of little Maddie. And often contemplates contacting social services on fearing for the safety of this child, and her ever perpetuating chances of finding herself in danger.

Maddie waddles down the path with her little bow legs, and hurries to the next street but one, to find that girl with the jet black hair who dispels the forlorn loneliness of her too long days. Again standing high on her tiptoes and with a stretching arm, she flicks the metal post flap of this front door with her fingertips, in highest hopes this particular child might just be at home. Maddie's heartbroken dejection is all too clear to the sympathetic mother of the girl, breaking the news her daughter is at nursery school, and won't be back until 3 o'clock that afternoon.

Wandering back to her Nana's house with her all-despairing frown, Maddie's round blue eyes light up on discovering an abandoned plastic doll on a muddy patch of grass. Almost all of its hair is cut awkwardly from its crown, and wears no clothes about it whatsoever. But the one arm it possesses is all she needs to happily carry her new companion along with her, holding its solitary hand.

"I'll take you home with me to Nana's house, but she isn't there much, you know," she says to her new friend, swinging it by both legs. "She goes to the bookies loads for the man who sells lollies, and he buys her beer for going in, as he isn't allowed anymore by the man in charge."

Kitty stands alert by her window, peering back and forth along the street, looking for topics for later gossip, and it isn't long until her calling is answered. She watches in utter disgust as a fridge is carried along the path from next door, followed by Maddie's Nana. Who stumbles drunkenly with her tatty looks and greasy complexion, and clad in that usual scruffy and over-stretched purple cardigan. She's handed some money from a shifty looking bloke in paint spattered wellington boots, who drives away in a dirty transit van coughing plumes of black smoke from its ancient exhaust.

Young Maddie looks almost too content as she waddles along the street, before turning up the broken stone path by the thick weeds and onwards to her Nana's door. On reaching upwards for the handle, Maddie is relieved to find it's now open. "There, I knew my Nana would be back at home." She calls out joyfully to the doll, "I can always count on her you know. I love staying with my Nana."

On stepping into the gloomy lobby, then pushing closed the back door, Maddie shivers. "Oh, it's nice to get warm when it's cold outside. I'll take you up to my room and we can play hide and seek, after we have something to eat for our tea." As Maddie steps into the kitchen, she looks around quite puzzled. "What's happened to the fridge? I'll ask Nana, she'll know."

Glancing around into this damp and poorly decorated living room, Maddie finds her Nana sprawled unconscious on the only sofa chair in the house. Picking up an empty super strength lager can, Maddie sighs, "Oh, Nana's drank too much beer again, and I won't be able to find out what's happened to the fridge now until tomorrow. Come on, we'll find something in the cupboard, I'm starving. Nana hasn't given me anything since those biscuits yesterday, or it might have been the day before." On glancing inside this damp and empty kitchen cupboard, Maddie tries her very best to hide her hunger and disappointment from her new friend.

Sitting on her dirty, urine soaked mattress, Maddie hugs her broken doll and begins to cry. Suddenly, a loud bang commands her startled attention as she looks towards the window. Where multi coloured explosions now trickle through the smoky air, illuminating this Bonfire Night's animated sky. And she gazes at this wondrous vision far away in the distance: beyond the sober reality of her own surroundings.

Maddie wakes the next morning with all of last night's wonders filling her little imagination. Again in that same dress, with the same clumps of dirty hair stuck to her face, she holds her doll up close by her ear, before responding to its muted conversation. "No, my Mam and Dad don't live here anymore. They were far too busy to look after me you know; so they wanted to live somewhere else without me being in the way. My Nana told me when I asked her, and she never tells lies. Come on, we'll go out and play, shall we?"

In her garden, Kitty smiles as she sees little Maddie hopping down the path and along the street with her doll in her arms, until she slowly disappears out of sight. As Kitty drops some rubbish bags into her dustbin, she's about to head back inside her neatly kept dwelling as Maddie's Nana soon catches her eye. She stumbles along the street from the opposite direction, before falling sideways into the splintered ruins of her rotten garden fence. Picking herself up with some effort, she now cautiously aims towards the house without dropping her carrier bag, containing several cans of super strength lager.

Kitty, scowling as her frustration boils over, decides that enough is enough. "Hey, Shambles! Where did your fridge go yesterday? And you neglect that poor little kid enough, don't you think? Do you even bloody bother trying to feed her? The poor little bugger looks like she's got rickets and just wanders the streets in her bare feet!.. Well?"

Lifting her head loosely from a drunken daze, Shambles slurs out, "Fuck off, Kitty, and mind your own business. What the fuck would you know about being lumbered with a bloody kid to look after, while the parents piss off abroad to live the life of riley! And I noticed nobody wanted a frigging baby with an ugly fat pig like you."

Kitty reddens in the face, ignoring that last piercing remark. "It's my bloody business where the lassie's involved. And I'll gasp my last breath before any harm comes to her. I've got my eye on you, Shambles, and God help me I'll report a cruel bastard like you to the authorities!"

Shambles rocks backwards, yelling, "I needed a drink, and there was fuck all in the fridge. And it's never been switched on for ages anyway, so I sold it... I'm going to bloody swing for you!" and Shambles makes an awkward lunge at Kitty, who thrashes out defensively, brandishing her dustbin lid.

"Hey! Just bugger off back to the bookies where you belong. You must be a part of the furniture in there, you drunken disgrace!"

Maddie roams the streets of Halstead Hill with her doll, as she talks happily for hours. "You are my special friend. And we're going to stay friends forever, you and me. Right until we are Nana's age..." And before she realises it, the day is steadily drawing to its close as Maddie stops for a moment. She gazes into some comfortable and warmly lit living room, where two worn out grandparents slept as soundly as the infant in a pushchair beside them. She stands forlorn in a sudden wind, stamping her cold feet as her tears slowly trickle.

A silver glint penetrates through her blurring teary vision as she uses the doll's one hand to wipe around her face. "Look down there! A new 50p piece. Shall we go to the shops and buy some sweets? I'm so hungry my belly hurts, come on!"

Pushing hard on the heavy door of Conrad Singh's Mini Market, Maddie goes inside.

"Hey, you! Your Nana owes me three pounds for what she stole," shouts Conrad, a bearded Indian man in an immaculate blue turban and white silk shirt. "How much money have you got there, you little sod?"

Maddie holds out her hand, sniffing hard on her runny nose. "Fifty pence, to buy some sweets for me and my friend."

Conrad flies out from behind the counter, grabbing for her hand. "This money will do for now, and you and your friend can get out of my bloody shop. And tell Shambles there'll be trouble when I catch her!"

Conrad snatches the doll from Maddie, while shoving her firmly out of the door, and throws it into the street. She waddles quickly towards it as a determined stray dog suddenly pounces, imprisoning this broken doll in its ever tightening jaws. And a struggle for her friend ensues, which by some miraculous effort, Maddie just barely wins. But the snarling canine snaps out, viciously sinking its bared teeth into her forearm. Several bystanders all fail to intervene on hearing Maddie's agonising cry; and on dropping the doll, she scurries back hysterically to the sanctuary of her Nana's house.

On returning home, Maddie finds her Nana in the usual chair, but with her face an unusually strange colour. And her sullen dark eyes without expression, but horribly wide open. Maddie takes several nervous steps back before her piercing screams carry throughout the house as Shambles slumps forward, crashing to the floor.

Next door, Kitty hears the commotion and quickly shuffles with all the speed she can muster. She arrives to find Shambles dead on the carpet, and Maddie on her knees crying frantically to her: holding out the raw wound of the dog bite, pleading for Kitty to help.

"I've lost my doll," cries Maddie.

As Kitty lifts the traumatised infant up into her arms she bursts into tears. "Oh god, you poor little mite! I pray for your sake you remember these things differently in the years to come, or better still, forget them altogether. Come on, dear, come with me, you're safe now." And here Kitty carries Maddie away, to call on the most crucial intervention of an ambulance and the police...

This emotional young couple cry tears of joyful relief on hearing their news: "There, I knew one day, just one day," whispers the man, struggling to compose himself, "that we'd get there eventually. And finally we've a little girl to call our very own. We've been blessed with a new beginning for us all, my love, and a fresh start for the future as a genuine family."

The young woman sobs as she holds a mannequin princess doll with long brown flowing hair, and a pretty yellow dress trimmed with gold. "I'm just so happy, can anything ever compare to this again? It's just happened all so fast, now I can't wait for her to arrive."

The man takes the doll from her and smiles. "I'm the same, I can barely hold on to my senses. But at last this doll we have kept so patiently in our desperate hope has a new owner, and we have a new daughter. And finally this doll has a name – it's Maddie's doll..."

This Stranger
in Black

These rapid droplets of rain trickle down the deep scarring across his cheeks while he stands on the windswept platform. His old suit soaks up the dampness in the air as he dusts away the water that has settled upon each shoulder. And it's true to say that this man, Tess Baxter, has often been described by many as a giant. But the moniker of 'wiry and lean' would also be as close a fit in description of his gait, as the gloves he wears on his shovel sized hands...

A quite unremarkable young man alights from a steam train with a brown leather suitcase as he looks around somewhat lost or disorientated. And his searching eyes soon settle upon the silhouette of Tess in the distance, as he hesitantly approaches this stranger in black.

With a smile broadening across Tess's craggy face, this youngster now gives his best effort to stand tall. But can scarcely reach the height of this drenched man's shoulder as he nervously introduces himself as Donald Jaggers. Tess laughs while reciprocating the gesture, and pats Donald on the back. 'I knew straight away that you were the dark haired lad I was to look out for. And if you're ready to go, the car is parked just around the back of the station.'

A Morris Minor car that has seen better days is the transport of choice for Tess, as he throws Donald's case onto the rug covered back seat. The engine is revved for some time before the grinding gears release a sudden and jerky trajectory along this bumpy cobbled road. Turning to his passenger, Tess comments, 'I hear, Donald, you've just recently turned twenty years of age.'

Nodding in response, this cautious kid mentions to Tess he just prefers the name 'Don'.

Tess concurs that 'Don' sounds good enough to him. And here this crouched driver tactfully broaches the subject and reasons for this kid arriving there to begin with. 'I had a phone call, Don, from your great auntie Isla. And she tells me she's very concerned with regards to your indifference, or acceptance, to the way you're treated by family and friends alike. And she fears if this carries on into adulthood, it could well pave your future with great difficulties.'

After beeping the horn at a careless driver for 'being up his arse', Tess asks Don to give him these details himself on what is concerning his auntie so much. For several moments the lad remains silent... Tess begins to whistle in an increasing pitch until young Don finally relents. So here he begins to explain to Tess how his family treat him as an inconsequential joke. And his friends intolerantly shout down and rubbish his consistently 'wrong' choices or opinions.

Nodding in agreement to everything this youngster now divulges, Tess vows that he won't be Mister Pushover 1965 for much longer. And in fact: 'It's all going to fucking stop!'

Don sits wide eyed for several seconds, stunned at hearing such a profanity from this man of the cloth.

Having no better response on hand, Don asks Tess how long he's been with the church.

'Too long' being the curt reply. 'Just keeping the Vassal Boys' Club up and running these days is quite enough for me.' And with the emphasis of this club being central to boys, Tess reminds Don, 'You're a touch too old for some of their activities. So you'll spend more time seeing the day to day arrangement of things.'

Don smiles, and contemplates these changes of scenery to be just as good for him as anything could in this unaccustomed situation...

The grinding gears of this worn Morris Minor make one last clatter as it takes its place in the parking bay of the Vassal club. Pulling his case from the back seat, Don looks around and up along a brick walled lane. There he sees a ragged and antagonistic ginger-haired boy arguing vehemently with his distressed and defeated mother. But stopping dead in his tracks, this boy waits while his parent takes several steps further ahead. And on turning to deter this railing child one last time, she forges on exasperated. Energetic with rage and frustration, this ginger terror makes a quick dash towards his mother, hoofing her hard up the arse with the scuffed toe cap of his boot. Where the impact is absorbed by the coarse and heavy fabric of the long and tattered coat she uniformly wears.

Don views this assault in a state of utter bewilderment. But Tess chuckles, while pointing out 'These little episodes are par for the course around Babel's Bay, and you'll soon acclimatise to it all'. And then locking up his car, Tess leads Don down several steps and on through the glass door entrance, beneath the weather worn banner of Vassal Boys' Club...

The scene inside is more like that of a school playground to Don. While random groups of chaotic young kids dart in all directions, Tess berates these 'Little bastards', shouting, 'You'll be out on your scruffy ears if you won't behave.' As Don is navigated through several more beige walled corridors, Tess lets him in on a secret: 'I do love these noisy shits really'.

After a sharp right turn, Tess stands with an arm outstretched and points to a window. 'This is the chapel, not than any fucker is ever in here, except for Dougie.'

Don observes through this small window a stout and balding man with a perpetual grimace, sniffing some powder from the lid of his tobacco tin.

'Is that Dougie?' enquires Don.

Tess nods his head, informing this youngster that the sniffing clergy is indeed his older brother, Dougie. 'He's supposed to help me with the administration and organization of things, but is all too often otherwise engaged.'

Don frowns as he asks what Dougie is sniffing.

'Fuck knows,' comes the reply. 'But if he can sniff it, smoke it, swallow it, or shove it up his arse, then Dougie's as game as a badger.'

Don barely contains his laughter as Tess slaps the lad on the shoulder, as his scarred cheeks widen along with his reassuring grin.

On asking Tess what else Dougie gets up to in his chapel, Tess divulges his brother sits on a pew mostly, just making weird noises.

'How did that all come about?' asks Don inquisitively.

And Tess enlightens Don further. 'My brother, the foolhardy tit, had once spent a lot of time over in Solomon's Quay. A place notorious for its residents dabbling in the occult; and over time, had supposedly acquired the skills to converse with angels. So now,

Dougie just sits in virtual darkness, apparently communicating with them all.' Though Tess remarks, 'It isn't so much the sounds of some heavenly consultation, but more of the old rasping bugger gargling with a gob full of loose phlegm.'

Don, now becoming even more curious, enquires on the whereabouts of this Solomon's Quay. 'Up Jack's arse and round the corner' jokes Tess, before explaining: 'It's actually the parish just across from the bay'. And here he takes young Don, and resumes his guided tour of this once old junior school.

On turning another identical corner, Don observes a concerned youth walking two injured young boys towards a wash basin. Tess stops while staring incredulously at a lad with a blood-smeared mouth, and then towards a smaller boy with an egg-shaped lump swelling up on his forehead.

'They've just collided,' says the oldest boy, as an already preoccupied Tess exhales heavily. 'Jesus wept,' he mutters under his breath, before resuming his quick and lengthy strides towards the next port of call.

Having now gauged Tess to be quite an approachable man, Don decides on discovering the origins of those deep and craggy scars across his cheeks. Tess, though slightly startled by this enquiry, still gives Don an honest response.

'There's this fucking wanker called Boz Jewitt,' Tess carries on. 'He's the resident hard-man who thinks he's made out of iron.'

Don's keen brown eyes scrutinise these wounds. 'Did he attack you?'

Tess shakes his head, telling Don it was an arranged fight umpteen years ago. And with Boz getting the living shit kicked out of him, he'd pulled a cutthroat razor.

'So what happened next?' asks Don.

With the appropriate riposte being: 'Well, you could say I'd never had a bigger fucking smile across my face'.

'I was partial to kicking fuck out of these "I'm untouchable" types. But I've long retired from removing my white collar to settle a score or two, having now reached that respectable age of fifty nine.'

Don, curious to know if Dougie assumes that same fiery temperament, requests more from his towering companion. Tess rubs his fingers across some fresh graffiti on a cracked plaster board. 'Dougie was a handy scrapper, but with that decrepit old goat being at the wrong end of sixty five, he's better off being for display purposes only.'

Eventually Tess shows Don to a dreary room scattered with several old camp beds that will become his humble dwelling for the foreseeable future. On regarding this room with obvious disappointment, Don's case is thrown by Tess, landing onto the least dirty and damaged bed. And it's here this clergy then proudly proclaims, 'Right lad, time for a fucking pint…'

As Tess strides confidently along a bungalow-lined road, Don hurries at speed also in his best efforts to keep up alongside. A hand rolled cigarette is then taken from a silver case by Tess, while the wind and dampness in the air make the lighting of it particularly awkward. But on deeply inhaling several puffs of smoke in through one side of his mouth, Tess blows a cloud downwards and in the direction of Don.

'That's got an unusual smell – where did you buy it?' And here Tess laughs, confiding to his curious friend it was given to him by his brother.

Don, being ever more intrigued, enquires where Dougie comes across this stuff as the aroma is quite nice.

'I've asked that old bugger myself,' Tess continues, 'but he just keeps repeating he finds little bags of it stashed away in the hymn book cupboard.' Don smiles a boyish grin, while Tess asserts his own belief. 'Those loveable little bastards at the club probably hide it there. Unaware that silly old fucker ploughs through the stuff as he gurgles and rasps away in the darkness of the chapel to his invisible angel mates…'

The Rook & Raven looks so bland to Don, and firmly stuck in World War Two as both he and his chuckling mentor step into the doorway of this sparsely populated pub. Tess, on walking directly across to the bar, asks the oafish landlord for 'two of the usual'. As each pint of thick dark ale is poured from some hand pulled tap, Don hears Tess shouting across the room in greeting to a man known as Isaac. Tess then nudges Don.

'Do you know why I call him that? Look at the size of his eyeballs; you could play fucking tennis with them.'

Don tries his best not to choke, as he stifles a laugh on taking his first sip from the pint glass. But thinking about Dougie, he quizzes Tess more. 'Is all of this angels and occult stuff real? Or just made up to scare people?'

Putting down his now nearly empty glass, Tess divulges his beliefs. 'Oh yes, Don. These forces are absolutely real. But I always make light of the notion in the company of any strangers, just for those who might be tempted by these darker arts. I've heard this stuff can reap some hellish consequences. Like the tale about some reckless young magicians along Solomon's Quay, many years ago.'

Before he can query this any further, Don sees Tess drain his glass dry and hurry away in the direction of the gents' toilets. On suddenly finding himself all alone, Don feels somewhat conspicuous as the scattered locals around the pub begin to scrutinize this young outsider.

Moments later Tess is back at the bar with wet, but neatly combed hair. 'That beer is off,' he says, telling Don he's just puked the whole lot back up. 'I just give my bracket a quick wash, and put the old mop back in place. Don't finish your pint, Don, or you'll spew up as well; let's fuck off somewhere else for another.'

The pub doors bang loudly as a thick set and middle aged man with a moustache strolls to the opposite side of the bar. He looks across to Tess as both men give one another a grudging nod of recognition.

'That's Boz Jewitt,' Tess says to a now nervous and jittery Don. 'The fucker who slit open my rosy cheeks with the razor.'

As this cautious kid suggests that now could be the right time to leave, Boz swaggers around the bar and immediately confronts Tess. 'Long time no see, eh. So what are you doing in here then, your holiness?'

Tess now towers even more upright. 'I'm having a pint with a friend, and would prefer to be left alone.'

Boz, stepping close into the face of Don, turns again to Tess. 'What, this fucking pipsqueak?' he says, while prodding Don forcefully in the chest.

On witnessing this act of arrogance, Tess decides to put Don's resolve to the test, reminding him of why he's here to begin with. 'Hey, I wouldn't take his bullshit. Get the twat told. He's treating you like you're nothing, exactly the same as how they would back home. And it's time it fucking stopped.'

Here Boz laughs incredulously. 'What? Is this fucking pipsqueak going to take me outside? Teach me some manners?'

Now Tess angrily rips away his white collar. 'If all you're looking for's trouble, then just say so, you fat cretin. You're not even fit enough to wipe my arse.'

As Don watches both men needle one another in this escalating argument, he begins to dwell on Tess's words. And then to every unquestioned liberty his friends and family had inflicted so casually against him. It's at this flashpoint his anger finally erupts. 'Hey, twat features,' he snarls to Boz, 'this fucking pipsqueak wants to take you outside.'

Here Tess grabs Don by the shoulders, and cautiously reminds him that Boz is a dangerous man, and to stand any chance of beating him, the kid will need his help. 'Thanks, Tess, but no. I need to do this alone, just to prove something to myself.'

Boz bursts into laughter as he takes off his leather jacket, while Don hastily pulls his woollen sweater over his head, and rolls up both shirt sleeves. And now Tess walks his agitated friend outside, and onto the slippery dampness of the muddy pub lawn.

Don stares intensely at Boz, who already awaits his opponent while laughing hysterically in disbelief that this idiot even dares to square up to him. On making a sudden lunge towards his foe, Don grabs Boz around the waist, pinning him tightly against the pub wall. And here both scrappers wrestle awkwardly while several ineffectual punches are landed by Don into the overhanging stomach of his sniggering tormentor.

Tess stands ready to intervene on this inexperienced lad's behalf as he watches Boz steadily getting the better of young Don. Yet still he remains at a distance, knowing the kid needs to fight for himself as a man: and to lose as a man if necessary.

Boz begins tightening his grip around Don's windpipe, as his pallor turns a deep purple. And in desperation, Don somehow manages to manoeuvre himself enough to knee his antagonist hard in the groin. Now releasing his grip, Boz suddenly finds himself falling flat on skidding over backwards. And here Don impulsively leaps into the air, drawing both knees upwards as high as possible, before stamping down hard onto the petrified features of his powerless prey.

As the soles of Don's shoes scrape across the bloody and ruined face of his victim, Boz falls unconscious. And on glaring murderously at this tragic tough guy, he jumps high into the air once again. This time he's grabbed mid-leap by Tess, who drags the kid clear.

'Fucking hell, I thought you were going to kill the bastard,' he shouts. 'We'd best scarper...'

And making a hasty retreat from the pub, Don comments, 'I actually enjoyed jumping on that twat's head; maybe too much. It's given me the faith to realise that I am actually capable of fighting back.'

Here Tess pats him on the shoulder. 'You went a bit overboard. But I did say that people getting away with treating you like shit was going to fucking stop. So now your homestead mob will have to find some other mug to slap down and bully. Won't they, Don...'

On returning to Vassal Boys' Club, Tess remarks, 'I've got a few things to sort out, kid. So why don't you stick your head in the chapel, to have a natter with Dougie? And get better acquainted.'

On feeling more confident than ever following his miraculous defeat of the local hard-man, Don agrees. And without warning, Tess bursts into a sprint, hot in pursuit of some boys up the corridor who'd tipped over the piano in the hall.

Quietly pulling open the chapel door with a degree of trepidation, Don watches this solitary silhouette with a shimmering illumination sitting alone in the barely lit room. For not having any clue what to make of this odd scenario, he feels somewhat of an intruder. But above all, he feels that something just isn't quite right.

'Don,' shouts a voice through a haze of that same aromatic smoke now so familiar to him. And here Dougie rises up slowly from his seat while taking several shuffling steps towards this trembling lad. 'We have a message, for you.'

Don laughs nervously, saying the only reason he popped his head in is because Tess had told him he should. Here Dougie reaches out, gently resting his gnarled, calloused old hands on Don's shoulders; where his entire body now tingles from a warm static surge.

With this unearthly glow encompassing him, Dougie's eyes flicker intently while he appears prisoner to an unnatural state of hypnosis. 'Uriel, the Archangel, speaks.' And here a powerful voice, yet gentle in tone, reverberates throughout the room. 'Don, beyond a fifth door you'll face a grave challenge, where your very soul will be dragged towards the abyss. And when the light compels you; call for us. And we will come.' Here several white flashes startle Don, along with Dougie's sudden collapse to the chapel floor.

Pulling open the door in a blind panic, Don shouts out for help, catching the attention of Tess who is passing by with a box of coloured files. He shakes his head exasperated.

'That daft old bugger hasn't keeled over again, has he? Christ, it's just a shame he can't levitate.'

And now relieved his mentor is here to take charge of this situation, Don begins helping Tess to carry Dougie over to the nearest bench. Where he now slumps limp in a heap, while snoring loudly.

With the time now fast approaching 10 o'clock, Don comments, 'I've just had a really strange experience, and feel all weird. So if it's okay with you, I'll head back along to my room for a snooze on one of those camp beds.'

Tess agrees that a good night's rest could be just what the doctor ordered. But also remarks: 'One thing you'll sharp realise, Don, is that every experience involving Dougie is, more often than not, quite strange'.

Lying propped up on several old and mouldy smelling pillows, the events of the day play on Don's mind. How his first real fight felt so invigorating that he swears to himself he'll never allow anyone again to treat him as they did. Safe in their knowledge there'd be no retaliation or reprisals whatsoever... And the glowing light around Dougie, and that voice in the chapel – 'Just what in hell was that all about?' Don thinks aloud. Surely it must be an elaborate joke being played on him... But finally, that lovely aroma of those funny cigarettes; it's something Don vows to himself that he must try whenever the opportunity arises...

The next morning Don feels quite refreshed, despite the chaos and fun from the previous day that kept him wide-eyed for what feels most of the night. But he soon realises he's overslept on hearing Tess's booming voice, shouting at some escaping kids for blocking the toilets with paper towels.

'Those little bastards, I guarantee I'll fucking swing for them one of these days,' he complains, while Don sticks his head out from around the door.

Now with Don up and about, Tess asks him if he fancies joining in some of the activities that occur on a daily basis. 'The sixteen year olds are just about to get going with the boxing and wrestling club. And after your little skirmish with Boz yesterday, this might be right up your street.'

Don muses on this idea for a moment, before nodding his head in agreement.

'Good lad, grab some shorts from the gym cupboard over there and follow me.'

The pungent smell from this gym hits Don before any physical activity ever can. Opening the doors he finds two pairs of lads sparring in a ring with drooping ropes, while others grapple competitively on a worn edged wrestling mat.

Tess shouts across to a short, stocky man in a red tracksuit. 'Hey Harry, this lad's called Don. He's never done this circuit before so go easy on him. I'll bugger off and pop back in later on.' And here Harry waves his hand in a beckoning gesture to a notably less hesitant Don, as he strolls across the floor towards him.

Almost an hour has passed by when Tess returns to the gym, to find Don experiencing that dense thud of this hard rubber mat, as he's speedily taken down with a leg trip. Tess beams with pride watching this once timid young kid coming out of his shell in such a short space of time. Don, on seeing his mentor now laughing so heartily, jogs across to inform him how much he's enjoying these physical activities.

'Great news,' says Tess, while slapping Don on the back. 'I think you're going to fit in here very nicely. I'll tell you what, go and have a hot shower and we'll pop round to the pub for a few drinks to celebrate.'

Don aches badly while taking this shower, as his adrenaline slowly subdues. But the rush of it all is becoming quite an addictive sensation. And so surprisingly to him, a one he's certainly looking forward to again tomorrow. But knowing Tess to be a thirsty man, and possibly just as thirsty as himself, he wastes no time at all in meeting him by the main reception desk...

Once again Don hurries along to keep pace with those giant strides of Tess. But suddenly this clergyman stops, and on opening his silver case, takes out another 'funny cigarette' specially hand rolled by Dougie. Tess turns his back to the wind and cups his hand to protect the flame of the lighter. Taking several deep puffs of this aromatic smoke, he offers it to Don. 'Have a couple of draws off this, kid; it won't do you any harm.' And here Don eagerly accepts Tess's offer without hesitation. And inhaling deeply on ingesting the smoke, he blows a thick jet of it upwards into the damp air...

On arriving at The Rook & Raven, Don suddenly begins to experience the subtleties of Tess's cigarette. A euphoric calmness washes over him for several moments, before some immediate paranoia and wide-eyed agitation overwhelm him. Tess laughs at the changing expressions in Don's face while asking him if he's okay.

'It's too much,' mutters Don, 'but challenging at the same time. I like it.' Here Tess throws his head backwards with laughter, while leading his protégé onwards by the arm.

These same elderly derelicts populate this place along with their vacant gazes just as they had the day before, while Tess and Don approach the counter. And it's here Tess purposefully castigates the disinterested landlord.

'Hey, I don't want another drop from those pumps until the lines are properly cleaned. I'm not getting bastard poisoned two days off the belt. So just give me and the lad a glass of your finest Sloe Gin.'

Here Don remarks that he'd never heard of this particular tipple before, but Tess assures him that it will go down very nicely.

As the landlord puts both glasses down before them, Tess picks up his drink and wishes his companion 'good health' as both fellows take their first sip of this pleasant refreshment. Tess nods knowingly, before asking Don what he got up to in the gym this morning.

'Oh, I tried out some punching combinations with a boxer on the hook and jab pads. And those wrestlers showed me some stretching routines and moves. I loved it. Boxing and wrestling are things I'd never imagined myself trying.'

Tess smiles. 'I knew a bit of rough and tumble would do you good. And I'm really proud of you, Donald Jaggers.' He carries on, with just a hint of a tear in his eye, 'You're a great kid. But have just had the misfortune in life to be surrounded by jealous or spiteful arseholes, who can only vent their destructive frustrations on a safe and easy target. And unfortunately, you became the self loathers' target of choice.'

At this moment, Don doesn't really know how to react to this genuine display of both affection and sincerity. 'Well thanks for taking me under your wing, Tess. I'm starting to feel like a different person already.'

Before Don knows it, another Sloe Gin is waiting ready on the bar for him while Tess downs another large glass like it's water. With somewhat of a fuzzy head, Don, feeling compelled to keep up with his mentor, drains his second glass in one straight gulp. Looking on with pride, Tess decides to give the youngster some advice. 'Don, as we know you've just turned twenty years old, and in my estimation have a great deal to offer this world. I once came to a crossroads in my life,' he continues, 'where I luckily chose the right path. And I think you might well be nearing a similar situation yourself. I won't hassle you, but what I'm getting at, Don, is a career like mine could be well worth considering. But whatever happens, always remember that what's meant for you will never pass you by.'

Don tries to make sense of this advice as the pub doors fly open. Boz Jewitt bursts in sporting bruised cheeks, black puffy eyes and a hideously deviated septum. 'Right, you fucking cunt! Get outside!' he screams to Don.

Tess begins pulling away his white collar while Don pushes his hand into the clergy's chest.

'No, remember I need to do this for myself. Nobody is taking liberties with me anymore. It fucking stops now, doesn't it, Tess?'

Tess looks to Boz, and then to his friend and smiles. 'You do whatever you have to do, kid, and I'll wait for you here.'

As Don paces towards this seething madman, a ceramic ashtray is hurled across the room, bouncing off Boz's face, slicing open his eyebrow. And on barely recognising this gaping wound, he pulls a shotgun concealed from within his long trench coat. Don attempts to push the weapon away as two shots are fired across the bar. And the spraying discharge of both barrels quickly overwhelms Tess, as he's thrown backwards and collapses to the floor.

Boz flees from the pub – having threatened the stunned locals to keep their mouths shut – and jumps into an awaiting car. While Don is struck numb with nausea, the landlord picks up the phone and dials 999 in a fluster, demanding an ambulance. On then hastily grabbing several beer towels, he does his best to stem these haemorrhaging wounds of the clergyman. As the concerned drinkers gather around him, Tess looks to Don, giving that same reassuring smile he always had. 'Well, that's me fucked,' he gasps. And on breathing a suddenly pained and final breath, he is gone.

Focusing on the motionless body of Tess, Don weeps for the loss of this man who taught him so much more than anyone could ever have. And recalling the final words of advice bestowed upon him by his mentor, Don recognises his newly liberated life has suddenly arrived at that very same crossroads. But now his decision of which path to follow requires no thought, and has without question, been well and truly made...

Trifle Toes

Seven year old Harry Transplant was chosen by his form tutor, a Miss Rinse, to represent his class in the 50 metres race at the infants' school sports day. With Harry having forgotten his plimsolls, he was curtly encouraged by his bossy teacher to run just in his socks.

On taking off his shoes, Harry lined up with the other three kids. And on hearing the school master's whistle, began scurrying ahead to the cheers around him. Holding his head high, and eyes tightly scrunched with exertion, he suddenly skipped a step, before two hops brought his race to a premature end. Looking to his right sock, he now found it heavy with the weight of the dog shit that had squashed through the thin white cotton and lodged between his toes.

Sitting down quickly as the others raced by to the finishing line, Harry pulled the sock away. Several nearby kids, on seeing the fudgy brown mess, began chanting 'Trifle Toes' again and again. Young Harry Transplant was devastated. He threw the sock in the air and ran towards the school cloakroom doors, to the laughter of Miss Rinse and the congregated teachers...

Frigging Trifle Toes: this name haunts Harry still to this very day. And on occasion of him being recognised by a face from those better best forgotten days of thirty years ago, their kids are readily encouraged to give a hearty shout of 'Trifle Toes' from across the street.

With his preference in life now to remain indoors and avoid all humiliation, Harry draws the heavy fabric curtains adorning his bedroom window as the sun slowly dims. And here settles down for the night as a suddenly painful and peculiar sensation wells in his throat.

While looking for some throat syrup, he attempts to cough as an odd shaped lump protrudes visibly through his gullet. And then swallows heavily to find the pain suddenly soothes away. On attempting to speak aloud, Harry is horrified to realise he has lost his voice. Though the voice he thought he'd lost is now moving its way down towards his stomach. Where he hears his own words quietly murmur from inside him.

In a blind panic, Harry runs to the mirror and attempts gasping out words that again emanate from his lively intestines. He grabs for his mobile phone to call the emergency doctor out; but realises it's impossible to communicate while a swallowed voice navigates its way around the deepest recesses of the gut.

As he scrutinises his own reflection, Harry grimaces. When his lips part, several healthy teeth fall from his mouth and scatter across the floor. On bending to pick them up, another cluster of teeth tumble out through his quivering lips. In his emotional and flustered panic, Harry's senses detect more murmurs and muffled sniggering. Grabbing around his stomach in horror, he realises this cacophony is now working its way around the bowel.

Harry's eyes are uncomfortably sore as he rubs them, while his vision becomes increasingly distorted and dim. On touching his now toothless mouth, his lips appear almost elastic around this ever tightening orifice. Having had more than enough of the weird goings on, Harry goes to bed convinced he must be dreaming. On turning out the light, he prays things will be back to normal tomorrow.

Harry can't settle as he tosses and turns, being driven mad by an uncontrollable itching in his anus. With an outstretched hand he runs his fingertips across what appears to be a set of teeth gradually protruding from around the sore sphincter. Crying out in distress, Harry freezes on detecting a soft murmuring directly from his rectum. He listens on attentively in a dreaded cold sweat, but just can't quite make out the words that appear to taunt him.

Sensing a crippling indigestion in his chest, Harry is very quickly taken by surprise as a foul tasting fart forces its way out through his painfully pursed lips. With terror filling his eyes, he begins to struggle as his now toothless mouth ceases of its own volition to give him breath. And instinctively flipping himself upright, he pelts towards the bathroom mirror.

This dreaded panic quickly dispels as he finds himself able to breathe once again. But to his horror, realises the rapid breaths emanate directly from his teeth rimmed anus. On reaching again towards his buttocks with a trembling hand, the teeth snap shut; biting hard the tips of his fingers. In a fit of outrage, Harry punches repeatedly between his bum cheeks; grazing his knuckles along the rough enamel edging.

After several moments of unnerving silence, Harry hears a faint and disturbing whisper from his backside: somehow sensing his earlier troubling thoughts. With a steady increase in pitch comes 'Trifle Toes, Trifle Toes, Trifle Toes!' – his arse just wouldn't shut its spiteful mouth.

On gripping the sides of his head in despair, Harry's thick brown hair begins dropping freely from his scalp to the floor. He struggles with his hideously blurring vision as he reaches to his eyes, finding a smooth layer of skin gradually healing over them.

Now grabbing blindly for both bath taps in a panic, and clumsily turning them on full, Harry pushes the chained plug in firmly as the gushing water splashes randomly around the room.

While stripping naked, Harry is tormented by the incessant goading of his cruel orifice. And climbing into the deep bath, he hesitantly squats downwards into the water. Once submerged above the waistline, he takes in several deep breaths through his gaping rectum. And here Harry slowly slips into unconsciousness, at the moment his mutated arsehole gurgles its final breath of 'Trifle Toes'...

Parental Guidance

He knows it's near his time. Just exactly how he knows is as much a mystery to him as anything cares to be to any particular person. Be it an extra sensory perception, or mere gut instinct; he is truly convinced by this recurring inclination nevertheless...

Terry is, and always has been, what many people consider a strange and uneasy person. The label of being 'backward' or 'simple' is consistently applied by those whose acquaintance with Terry is little better than their own considered intimacy with the man in the moon. Yet, the judgements imposed from his self appointed 'betters' flow as freely as wine.

As a young boy, Terry Tallow and his parents were unfortunately involved in a dreadful car accident. A skidding truck in the wrong place at the wrong time hit the family car head on. Terry's mother often hounded this shy infant into wearing a seatbelt for his own wellbeing, which he always did; though fatally for them both, his parents did not. Terry, being the lone survivor of this homely, conventional family, was diagnosed with an incurable brain trauma: leaving every subsequent situation in his life an overly complicated or frightening prospect.

Being 58 years of age, Terry lives in a supposedly adequate bedsit which he has occupied for most of his adult life. Deemed as fit to inhabit alone by the authorities who placed him there, on their assumption he consumes his erratically prescribed medications. A pleasant district nurse visited Terry weekly. But with health department cutbacks, now frequent themselves to occasion only. And the apparent keeping an eye on his mundane activities no longer included his medicinal essentials, now taken only sporadically.

On his Victorian looking sideboard, one of the few furnishings of this poorly decorated room stands a decaying photograph of Terry and his mother. This being their last holiday together at Cleethorpes before her life was tragically taken. Pining away in his loneliness he holds the silver framed image tightly to his cheek. Tearfully reminiscing about this doting matriarch he idolises so much. With his only ambition in life being: to be just like she was.

Wandering the usual streets in the usual order forms the tapestry of Terry's days. He stops by each phone box in turn jamming his fingers into the returned coins flap foraging for any discarded change; a hobby filling his time enough to see out the dragging day. The last few weeks see Terry more despondent and unhappy than usual. With his frequently troublesome indigestion initially easing, he remains dutifully convinced his time is soon to be up; never to experience unwarranted solitude and misery any longer.

He's highly unlikely to miss the gang of kids who hang around outside of his multi patronised dwelling; always bullying Terry as he waits for the ice cream van to stop so he can buy a few bags of his favourite KP cheese & onion crisps. The leader of these being some 12 year old, podgy, waddling coward from the neighbouring affluent estate, named Benjy. He sees his shy target as easy prey: while himself being infamously renowned for steering clear of any rough kids spoiling for a fight.

This mollycoddled young upstart aggressively pesters Terry for his money with the full support of the pack. Insisting he must be loaded on account of him being just a 'daft fucking spastic', as everyone knows 'fucking spastics' get money chucked at them. Terry threatens these kids with the police for always harassing him. Benjy confidently retaliates with the warning that the kids will inform the police Terry is a paedophile, offering sweets from the ice cream van in return for touching them. A situation endured through this victim's sad eyes being clearly a hopeless one.

Getting back inside his bedsit in this damp old house, Terry rubs his pained chest and sits on the edge of his bed while looking tearfully at his mother's photo, and across to the spacious old wardrobe. On standing up he opens its weighty doors, and taking out the one item neatly hanging in it, begins dutifully changing into his attentively preserved nurse's uniform. This all being quite a remarkable transformation in comparison to his distinctive brown corduroy trousers and green woollen polo necked jumper that drape a barely varnished wooden chair.

Climbing into the heavy blanketed bed, Terry coldly shivers before curling up in prayer. Sniffing back his defeated emotions in the darkness, he endures several restless moments before finally dropping off to sleep.

Terry wakes the next morning before the sun rises, methodically changing into his outdoor clothes on finding his bearings. He nervously scurries down the creaky, barely lit staircase he always believes to be haunted – which his alcohol-ravaged neighbours convince him of when trying to scare him witless – before leaving the bedsit behind as the sun casts a dark red glow on its slow peaking above the horizon.

On the usual route of his day, Terry shoves his fingers into the returned coins flap of the phone box along the High Street. On hearing a dull and dense thud just outside, he quickly turns to find an old lady has taken a turn for the worst and fallen. Terry is roughly jostled out of the way by some impatient bystanders, believing their intervention to be of superior value to his own. Here he desperately attempts lunging to this disorientated lady's assistance, but awkwardly ends up hindering the incident rather than helping. Helping, though, is all he wants to do. Knowing this is exactly what his mother would have done in this situation had she been there, and done it far better than any of those 'stupid flipping idiots'.

Agitatedly shuffling his feet on the way home, Terry angrily mumbles to himself about those 'horrible blinking twits' who wouldn't even give him the time of day. He now more than ever wants his time to be up, again rubbing away at the nuisance indigestion on his chest. He found the chance he'd been waiting for, to be just like his mother, and those 'smelly twerps' took it away from him. Terry then blows his congested nose noisily on his eyes brimming full with lamenting tears.

Watching from his painted shut bay window, Terry looks down onto the street below and sees the arriving ice cream van. With no signs of the gang, he decides to scurry in a pained and panicked groan down these horrible stairs, with the purpose of buying some crisps with the handful of coins he has left in his money jar secretly kept under the bed.

As this nervous customer approaches, the driver sniggers contemptibly while sliding back the glass panel window. On Terry asking for the crisps, this gum-chewing, arrogantly confident prick casually throws the bags down onto the counter before him. Sarcastically enquiring whether he needs a plastic ice cream spoon to eat them with. Terry, on confusingly replying he doesn't eat crisps with a spoon, hears a loud chorus of jeers and laughter behind him. This dreaded gang suddenly appear; all intent on joining the callous mockery. Terry quickly turns several times in an agitated manner, shouting at everyone to 'flipping stuff off'. Here Benjy spitefully encourages his mob to 'fucking spit on the gonk'.

On forlornly turning a fiddly key in the lock of his bedsit door, having again hastily navigated the unnerving shadowy staircase, he maintains his disappointed frown on stepping inside the room he was never once been heard to call his home.

The tattered 1980 Beano Annual always makes Terry laugh on reading it over and over. On feeling the urge for cheering up, this old book usually does the trick; but somehow tonight is just different. On approaching the enormous wardrobe he again changes into his immaculate nurse's uniform; scrutinising his smartened appearance in the wardrobe mirror before pulling back the heavy blankets of his bed. Looking to the calm inducing image of his mother on the sideboard, he emotionally curls up in prayer before finally drifting off to sleep.

Wakening in the night with a sharp jolt, Terry panics as his sweating body quickly stiffens on finding himself unable to breathe. For too many terrifying moments his attempts of gasping out for help are fruitless.

Suddenly there is absolute nothingness, an intangible emptiness replacing the void where an unhappy and unfulfilled life once lived.

The touch of a gentle hand glides across his brow. Terry opens his eyes to find his mother attentively leaning over him. Still dressed in the same nurse's uniform she wore while being cut from the wreckage on that awful day she was killed. All of Terry's pain and heartbroken loss is gone, now replaced by an indescribable euphoria.

Looking down upon her son with that compassionate soothing smile, she gestures towards the warmly illuminated bedsit doorway. On taking the joyous, and suddenly so youthful Terry's hand, he lifts without effort from the bed. With that misplaced emotion of a trusting infant's love overwhelming him again, she gently leads her boy away; as peacefully together, they pass through into the light...

Somewhere Else

Sometimes I just need a walk. Shake off the darkness, and free my thoughts into the light of day. I love this place; though I'm not quite sure where I am. I've never known how I find my way here; it's one of those places where I just end up.

It's ten past six in the morning, but the even earlier rising sun makes this place so welcoming. A warm breeze meanders its way through long coarse grass just down past some old rusted railings. They separate me from the clear and desolate river as it passes me quietly by.

To my left are derelict dock buildings, still throwing shadows of the long gone trades and crafts of a time far less complicated. I feel so happy here; care-free. I can't hear a single sound while walking such a peaceful road... This I will forever remember: why can't things always be this way?

On passing a bend I see a sprinkling of friendly looking faces waiting outside a pub. An old Victorian exterior, and so endearing in every way: though, somehow lonely and lost; with just the ghosts of its past to remind it of the many friends who once kept it company there.

One of these friendly faces, a seemingly modest man, begins to talk with me. He asks me that with the pub soon opening, would I care to go inside for a beer... It's only just gone twenty past six, but as fate has brought me here again for a reason – and knowing nothing this idyllic can last forever anyway – I agree.

Soon enough the pub doors open and more people begin to show. Everyone is so genuine and pleasant: why can't things always be this way... The landlord greets us all with open arms; as welcoming as the interior of this charming little pub.

When everybody has a drink and gets themselves comfortable, the heavy curtains are drawn as a large white projector screen slowly lowers behind the bar. I stand there with some of these friendly faces and feel quite excited by the anticipation of others for what is to come.

The projector starts up and a very old black and white film lights up the screen. The picture is rounded at the corners, a bit grainy and runs at twice the speed. Nothing to get excited about really. It's set in the day when horses pulled beer kegs on carts, and straw hats and aprons with rolled up shirt sleeves were worn by the draymen.

One sturdy drayman stands proudly on some cobbled lane as smartly dressed chattering on-lookers congregate nearby. A powerful black Shire horse trots down towards the end of this lane pulling an empty cart; slowing to a stop on reaching its trusted master.

Suddenly from his side, this bearded butcher lifts high an enormous meat cleaver, forcefully chopping the gleaming blade deep into the horse's shoulder as it staggers sideways in shock. The grouped bystanders beam in delight as this animal's brutal dismemberment begins.

I turn from the screen. I can't watch as everyone about me appears entertained by this horrible sight. I don't belong with these people. I have to get out of this now sickening place. I calmly try the main door, but it's locked. One of the still friendly faces seems puzzled by what I've done, and tells me there are more films still to watch. I say I want to leave; everyone overhears me. They stop and glare: the mood suddenly changes. Something feels horribly wrong. I don't want it to be like this anymore...

A Heart of Thorns

Missy's heavy, thudding footsteps quickly close in on young Alexander Villiers as he pelts across the deserted school yard. And with each panic filled gasp of air he inhales, those black coffee coloured eyes fill to the brim with tears of terror...

'Alexander! Get here now,' shouts Missy with a heavy panting breath. 'It'll only be worse for you if you don't stop, you skinny prick!'

Alex runs regardless, and still as quickly as he can. 'Fuck off, Missy. You fat cow,' he shouts as his legs suddenly fail to carry him any further.

'Right, you shit little bastard, you're in for it now!' pants Missy.

Alex, in a fit of panic, pleads desperately as his pursuer now grips him ever tighter by his school tie. 'Why is it always me you hit, Missy? I'm only ten, and you leave school in two weeks!'

Missy sneers arrogantly, 'I hit you, Villiers, because I fucking can! Now say your prayers.'

All pleas fall on deaf ears as Alex begins to feel the relentless torrent of heavy clenched fists raining down onto his back.

On dropping to his knees and curling into a ball, Missy kicks hard into her victim's ribs as Alex squeals and whimpers. Trying hard not to choke on these tears, Alex cries, 'I'll get you back, Missy, I'll never forget.' And following three vicious kicks to the side of his head, young Alex begins to lose consciousness...

A car horn abruptly wakes Alex from his troubling daydream. Those school yard beatings of twenty five years ago should be an almost forgotten memory, but to him they remain as fresh and vivid in 2006 as if they had occurred only yesterday.

Alex adjusts his bleary eyes as he stares out of the net curtain draped bay window. 'Ah, good man, there's Sam and it's three o'clock on the dot. How does he still manage it?'

The door bell is already ringing as Alex makes his way to the varnished oak front door, and opens it.

'Hey Alex, it's good to see you again, my old chum,' says Sam, dropping his holdall while wiping his feet methodically on a rubber edged mat, and shaking his old friend's hand with vigour.

Alex laughs. 'A whole weekend together, eh? Just like the old days.'

Sam also can't hide his joy – 'And what better way to do it than to visit my best friend Alex.'

On Alex declaring they will both have to get extremely pissed, Sam stands relaxed, with both hands on his hips.

'Oh, I fully intend to,' he says. 'I'll pop down to the Off Licence later on before it gets dark, but let me have a sit down first. My legs are aching after all that driving.'

Alex smiles and begins to mock Sam. 'Yes you can have your sit down, you poor lamb.'

Sam laughs, grabbing his holdall and follows Alex into his wood beamed, spacious sitting room.

They sit for a few moments now silently contented, and in the comfort of some plush leather reclining chairs.

'So,' smiles Sam, 'I believe congratulations are in order.'

Alex looks across to his friend. 'They are indeed. But which aspects of my illustrious career are you congratulating me on?'

Sam shakes his head in amusement. 'You're a daft sod. All hail big head Mr Villiers! You know I mean the aerospace job.'

Alex feigns a confused look for a second. 'Oh, that. Yes, it is rather nice. To be honest, Sam, I really didn't believe I stood a chance. It's an executive's post, but a lot of it's contract based, so I'm not home and dry just yet.'

Sam listens intently, nervously biting his thumbnail. 'Yeah, but if the contracts do go through, Alex, will there be any openings suitable for me at the company?'

Alex tells his friend he's more than confident he can find him a decent position.

'Ah, lovely stuff,' sighs Sam. 'I was hoping you could pull a few strings for me. The missus wants the place redecorating, you see.'

Alex stands ponderously for a moment. 'Maybe I can speed things up for you somewhat. I'll just give a colleague of mine a quick ring; he's never let me down yet.' As Alex picks up his phone, it begins to ring in his hand. 'Oh, bollocks, who's this; I don't recognise the number.'

'Oh, well... Hello!' A few moments of silence pass by while Alex's expression is one of increasing bewilderment. 'Missy Mullins! You're not looking for a punch bag, are you?' Alex scrunches up his face in his difficulty to hear this voice clearly. 'My number was on who's phone? I'm not being funny, Missy, but of all people, why ring me?'

Alex wanders to the window, where he always stands to think. 'Yeah, we do go back a long way, and yes I do remember, but you want us to go where?' Now staring at the dark orange afterglow from a setting sun, Alex carries on, 'I quite agree the burying of the hatchet is long overdue. But us both doing that by attending a bare knuckle fight! Jesus, that's a bit heavy, isn't it?' Feigning humour, Alex enquires if this isn't setting up round two for them both, as he sits down opposite Sam while rapping his fingers on the chair arm.

'It will be good to clear the air, Missy. But my friend is here for the weekend, and he's quite the pacifist.' Sam looks at Alex with a furrowed brow, as his friend continues, 'I'll do my best to talk him round though, but I can't quite promise anything.' Alex appears eager to end this conversation as his speech quickens. 'Yes, Jaggers Barn at the far side of the Feetham Fields at eight o'clock tomorrow. Okay Missy, might see you there... bye.'

Alex stands and wanders the room for a few seconds, incredulous to the conversation he's just had. 'Jesus Christ, Missy fucking Mullins. Who would ever have guessed it?'

Sam finds himself none the wiser, asking if this name is a one he should recognise.

'Maybe I have mentioned her to you, Sam,' says Alex, lost in his thoughts. 'The strangest thing about it all is I was thinking of her just earlier, only seconds before you arrived.'

Here Sam enthusiastically blurts, 'Ooh! And what have you been up to, you dirty devil, tell me more!'

'Now, now, Samuel Bagwell, this is not what your prurient imagination is conjuring.'

Sam looks at Alex with his sudden enthusiasm somewhat deflated. 'Mr Villiers, ladies and gents. Here he is: the world's biggest party pooper, who won't let the dog see the rabbit.

'Come on, Alex, who is Missy fucking Mullins? You've got me curious.'

Alex stretches his arms high above his head, enquiring, 'How do you fancy going to a bare knuckle prize fight tomorrow, Sam?'

'No I do not,' Sam replies sternly. 'And who is Missy?'

Alex lifts his head from side to side, then up and down 'Missy is someone I had almost forgotten about, from a time I would rather forget. If you agree to pop round to the shops soon for the vodka, I'll tell you all about her.'

Sam comments that if Alex comes completely clean about Missy, he'll even consider going to 'that godforsaken fight' tomorrow. And here Sam extends his hand to Alex, who shakes it firmly on their gentleman's agreement. And now sitting back in the comfy chair, Sam places his hands behind his head in readiness for the tale about Missy. 'Right, I'm all ears.'

'You know how every school has a bully, Sam?' Who then silently nods in agreement. 'Well, I had my own personal bully who punched and kicked me so hard that I would often pass out. And the only reason she did this is because she could... Her name was Missy Mullins.'

Sam sits forward, wide eyed with shock. 'Bloody hell, Alex! Is that who you were speaking to on the phone just then?'

Alex looks almost hypnotised as he follows the swirling patterns of his carpet. 'Yes, Sam, the very same.'

Squirming in his seat, Sam becomes increasingly uncomfortable. 'Then I believe you should have nothing more to do with her. She could still be a nasty piece of work, and I don't want you in trouble if she starts that business again.'

'No, no, bloody hell, Sam, it's all just water under the bridge for me now.'

Sam claps his hands, rubbing them together. 'Good man, I'm very glad to hear it. I always say that holding a grudge against someone is like you taking the poison and waiting for the other person to pop their clogs.'

Alex smiles at Sam, nodding his head in agreement. 'Yes, poor Missy had some rotten luck in the years following school. She had twins to a fellow named George, who apprenticed at Gunnar's Butchers on the High Street.'

Sam listens on, but impatiently queries as to where the rotten luck arrives into the situation. Alex looks directly ahead with this sombre reflection. 'Very soon after the twins were born, George had an accident while slicing some meat, and severed an artery. He was alone in the shop at that point, lying there until he bled to death.'

Sam sits horrified as Alex continues his tragic tale. 'Within days of George's death, the twin girls, on their very first birthday suddenly went insane overnight;

frothing at the mouth. The poor things have been locked away for some years now in a secure mental institution.'

Sam, looking almost teary with compassion, tells Alex he is so pleased they can finally bury the hatchet after all, considering the tragedy of his harrowing story.

'Well, there you have it, Sam, that's the legendary saga of Missy. So are we going to watch that fight tomorrow then? We did shake on it.'

Sam hurriedly explains that it's not really his scene at all. As Alex quickly interrupts, reminding his friend, 'Come on now, we shook on it, Mr Bagwell... We shook on it!' Sam glares with a fit to burst irritation, commenting, 'Well I hope it's all over and done with bloody quickly, that's all I'm saying.'

Alex chuckles loudly while slapping his friend on the back. 'Good man. Do you fancy going for that vodka then, Sam?'

And on nodding his head with a beaming smile, Sam confirms he most certainly does. On asking Alex if he wants mixers with his drink, it's quickly decided by both to give their best efforts at 'drinking each other under the table'. And Sam laughs readily while making his way out of the creaking front door, and closing it firmly behind him.

Wandering over to his bay window, Alex watches Sam crossing the quiet road. On reaching the other side, his friend suddenly stops, turning to see the silhouette of Alex at the window. And here Sam sticks high two fingers, before hurrying off along the road.

Alex laughs and shakes his head, while reaching across to a shelf on his elaborately carved bookcase, and picks up an unboxed pack of Aleister Crowley Tarot cards. Sitting down at his dining room table, Alex splits the pack into the suits of cups, wands, pentacles and swords. He then deals them into a ten point formation, familiar to him as The Tree of Life. And there studies these esoteric cards as his eyes close for several minutes in deep meditation.

Suddenly Alex jolts upright out of his trance, as Sam taps away at the door. 'Come on, Alex! Open up! I've procured a bottle of the good stuff here, from Mister Conrad Singh at his Mini Market.' On Alex opening the door, Sam brushes past him while heading for the kitchen. He quickly turns on the almost blinding halogen light while opening a high cupboard door, and peers around for two glass tumblers.

During this eager commotion, Alex grabs a tray of ice from his tall chrome freezer and drops several cubes into each glass. This is followed by Sam then filling the glasses with the freshly opened spirit. Chinking their glasses together, the friends take their first sip.

'This should see us right for the rest of the evening,' says Sam. 'This was their biggest bottle, a litre or more I should think.'

Taking another sip, Alex coughs with its biting undiluted strength. 'A triumph, Samuel, a triumph. Let's have a sit down now, eh? In case we start falling over with the power of this stuff.'

Sam chuckles as he wanders into the sitting room first, and approaches the table where the Tarot cards are still neatly lain out, just as Alex had left them. 'Oh, no Alex, you aren't still into all of that picture card stuff, are you? I thought you'd left all of that weird mumbo jumbo behind years ago.'

Alex, already now seated, nonchalantly looks across to the table. 'Oh those, yeah, I was just looking at them while you were at the shop; I haven't touched them in years.'

'Good,' says Sam, slightly relieved. 'Hey, do you remember how you first got mixed up in that new age stuff; a leisure centre of all places.'

'Yes, Sam, I remember it like it was yesterday. We virtually lived in that place fifteen years back, while we shared that old flat in Gabbitas Terrace.' Alex smiles and looks to the usual window, again so deep in thought. 'I can see it now, and the one thing we both enjoyed more than anything was a good game of squash.'

Alex recalls that old familiar ricochet sound of a bouncing rubber ball, and he's immediately transported back there once again. In a squash court at Church Park leisure centre, breathless and drenched in sweat, now standing face to face with his best friend, Sam...

'Well, come on, you cheating sod,' goads Sam. 'That ball was definitely over the red line.'

Alex adjusts the strings on his racquet while feigning ignorance. 'Okay, okay, we'll just play for that point again then, Mr Fuss.'

Sam laughs while hurrying his friend. 'Come on, we've only got about a minute left, and this is the decider.'

Alex bounces the hot rubber ball while listening to the frantic efforts from the courts around him.

On hastily serving this ball from within his box, its trajectory hits above the red line.

'Out,' shouts Sam, while Alex retrieves the ball from the far corner.

On kneeling down to catch his breath, Alex looks to the glass wall where two attractive long haired young women pass by. They pause for a second, looking to Alex, and giggle girlishly before walking on.

Alex can't hide his interest, and beckons to Sam. 'Did you see those two delightful young foxes?'

Sam can't hold his laugh in any longer. 'Oh, bloody hell! It's lothario Villiers, on the loose again.'

Alex remains buoyant in his enthusiasm. 'Do you not fancy catching them up, and having a chat then?'

Sam begins wiping down his face with a blue hand towel, while surprising Alex with the revelation that he had met someone a couple of weeks ago. And wanted to wait and see how things worked out with her first.

'Oh,' says Alex, 'who's the dark horse, eh?'

Sam smiles while opening the glass court door. 'Well, that's me all done; I'm popping downstairs to get a shower and I'll leave you to your foxes.' And here Alex pulls the cover over his racquet top, waving with it in the direction of his friend.

Sam has just finished getting dried. And with his towel around his waist, stands in front of the steamed up mirror and begins combing his mousey blond hair. He places it, as he always does, into the neatest parting that anyone could wish to own. He flexes his muscles for all of their worth, but remains ever disappointed by the results.

Here Alex bursts into the changing room, still in his black tracksuit bottoms and vest, while throwing down his old sports bag.

'Bloody hell, Sam,' laughs Alex. 'Those two are Witches!'

Sam stops for a moment in puzzlement. 'Who are Witches?'

Alex, in his giddiness, grabs Sam tightly in a side headlock, while ruffling his freshly combed hair. 'Those two femme fatales who passed us both while we played squash, Penny and Jasmine. They said they are Witches. They're having a coffee in the canteen – do you not fancy it?'

'Piss off!' snaps Sam, as he wriggles free, all red in the face, and combing his hair once again. 'No, I'm okay,

Alex. I'll just head back to the flat as I've a few things to do anyway.'

Alex takes off his vest just as Sam walks by him to leave. And here playfully slaps him hard across his exposed back. Alex cries out, recoiling in pain as Sam flies out of the door with a boyish chuckle, encouraging his friend to be a good boy.

Alex bounds his way up the stairs to the canteen where he's overpowered by some indelible aroma of a tangy brown sauce, and vinegar over hot chips. He listens to the myriad sounds about him. Numerous shrieks from the playful kids in the busy leisure pool, along with the lifeguard's whistle all melt into one another in the too humid air. He sees Penny and Jasmine still sitting at the table where he left them, sipping at their coffee cups. As he so confidently strolls over towards them, Penny sees him approaching and nudges into Jasmine while they excitedly whisper to one another.

'Hello again, Girls,' beams Alex.

'Hello again, Alex,' gushes Penny. 'Why don't you sit down and join us?'

Alex points his finger towards his chest, grinning. 'I can't be keeping company with a couple of Witches, people might start to talk.'

'We are Wiccans, Alex,' says Jasmine. 'We only told you we were Witches to freak you out, for a joke, you know?'

Alex bursts into a brief nervous chuckle, while sitting down next to Penny and looking directly across to Jasmine opposite. 'Oh, well pardon me, Wiccans, but is there that much difference between your good selves and a couple of Witches, then?'

Penny smiles. 'Well why don't you join in with us and find out? We'll be here again tomorrow after our aerobics class if you're interested.'

Alex nods his head agreeably. 'Sounds delightful. I shall make every effort to attend.'

'What about your friend?' asks Jasmine. 'Where is he anyway?'

Alex ponders her enquiry for a second, before responding, 'Oh, Sam. He's head over heels with a girl he's just met. And possibly just a little under the thumb in my estimation.'

Jasmine leans in close to Alex from across the table. 'There is something strange about you, Alex.'

He stares on blankly as Penny bursts into a fit of giggles. 'Yes, hasn't he got a handsome and distinguished look about him for such a young man?'

'No,' says Jasmine, looking quite serious for such a usually upbeat girl. 'It's your eyes, Alex. I've never seen such dark and haunted eyes.'

'Well, that's especially nice of you to say so, Jasmine,' grins Alex.

'No!' she asserts. 'It's not supposed to be a compliment.'

Alex, feeling rather flat and insulted, replies, 'Well thanks so very much. There's nothing like starting as you mean to go on, eh?'

Jasmine leans back in the chair while folding her arms. 'An unfulfilled vengeance haunts you, does it not? It's all in your eyes, Alex. They tell nothing whatsoever to those without vision, but I can truly see.'

Alex turns his bewildered gaze from Jasmine, and looks to Penny. 'Well, ladies, this has been an education. But it's time I made a few tracks and headed home; see what Sam is up to. What time should I be here tomorrow, Penny, if it's still okay?'

'It is still okay,' replies Penny. 'Be here for two o'clock. And don't let Jasmine put you off.'

Jasmine watches on silently, and rather un-amused.

'Okay Wiccans, I'll bid the both of you a very good day.' And Alex pushes himself upright at the table, and wanders out of sight.

Thinking about Penny gives Alex a definite spring in his step on making his way back along the plainest row of gardenless houses that only Gabbitas Terrace could provide. A long and neglected street lined with old front doors on pavements, accompanied by the incessant echo of a dog's distant bark. And a child's broken pram with three wheels mounts a discarded piss-stained mattress lying close to the dirty back lane. And on arriving at number 66, Alex puts his key into the lock of this forsaken one bedroom flat he shares with Sam; and on turning the key, steps inside.

'Ah, Alex, how did it go with the Witches then?' asks Sam eagerly.

'Oh, it went okay, Sam. Penny is lovely, but Jasmine only seems to look right through me. It's just really difficult to explain her stare.'

Sam jokily wiggles his fingers at Alex. 'Beware! She's reading your soul, Alex, beware!'

Alex smiles with a faint trepidation in his expression. 'Well, it's funny you should say that.'

'Say what?' asks Sam.

'Oh, nothing,' Alex replies dismissively. 'I fancy some vodka. Does one care to join me?'

Here Sam puts his hand to his chin, feigning a studious look. 'Now, one is talking my kind of language.'

The next day, an hour of lifting weights in the gym passes Alex by virtually unnoticed. With his mind now firmly fixated on meeting Penny again at two o'clock, everything else was purely peripheral. When the time reaches one thirty, Alex takes a shower and methodically preens his coarse black hair with gel. Following a generous splash of aftershave, he throws his sports bag into a dented wall locker, and is finally ready.

Alex springs up these same rubber edged steps, finding Penny and Jasmine seated exactly where he had left them just the day before; in that same humid air, and that same myriad of sounds and aromas about him as he approaches their table.

'Hi Wiccans, have I arrived a touch too early?' asks Alex.

Penny jumps up to her feet while Jasmine remains firmly seated. 'Alex, it's nice to see you're here, and you can never be too early,' she gushes. 'Why don't you take a seat?'

'Well, I don't mind if I do,' replies Alex, as he sits down in an orange plastic chair.

Jasmine looks across to Alex, again making no effort to conceal her scrutiny of his haunted eyes. 'Penny Goldman,' barks Jasmine, 'I think we should start by informing Alex of my Wiccan status. That when in a coven, you address me as High Priestess.'

Alex stifles a chuckle. 'High what?' he asks incredulously.

'Excuse me, Alex,' says Jasmine sternly, 'we both take the religion of Wicca very seriously. Becoming a High Priestess is a duty not to be taken lightly.'

Alex on realising the gravity of her commitment utters, 'Oh I'm sorry, Jasmine, but I have to say this Wicca stuff is all new to me. There's certainly no offence intended, and I offer my apologies.'

Here Jasmine frowns grudgingly. 'Apologies accepted, Alex.'

'It's just that when I was a kid,' Alex carries on, 'stuff like this was only for Hallowe'en, that's all. So again I apologise.'

Jasmine smiles with a more relaxed manner. 'Well, Alex, we, as in Wiccans, call Hallowe'en Samhaim. But it's pronounced Soween; it's a Sabbat.'

Here Alex's face contorts with confusion. 'A Sabbat?'

Penny smiles as she watches this all unfolding before her. And she combs through her long brown hair with her fingers. 'Yeah, Alex, I found it all difficult when I first started. Jasmine initiated me into the Wiccan circle last Beltane; and I was May Queen for the day.'

Alex raises his eyebrows with no further intentions to offend. 'May Queen sounds great.'

'Well,' enthuses Penny, 'there's twelve of us in the coven so far, but really we need thirteen. How about it then, High Priestess?' she says excitedly, looking to Jasmine. 'Alex could even be our High Priest one day.'

Jasmine lowers her head pretending not to hear, while the flowered garland in her hair slips slowly down her forehead, and comes to a halt on covering her eyes.

Penny quickly turns her attentions back to Alex. 'So, do you fancy hanging around a while?'

Here Jasmine quickly interjects. 'Penny, you know we need to discuss the upcoming Esbat celebrations with the waxing of the Moon.'

And Penny sighs despondently as Jasmine pulls a small pamphlet from her pink leather sports bag.

'Alex, I've brought this for you.' He reaches out his hand while enquiring what it is. 'It's a brief introduction to Wicca, if you are serious about this. Have a read through it and see what you think. We won't be here tomorrow, but will be the day after; same time and place.'

Penny and Alex beam to one another in their close proximity. 'That sounds fine, Jasmine. And I can only say thanks for the invitation, girls, it's been quite an education.'

As Alex begins to walk away, Penny gives a final 'Bye' with a satisfied grin on her face.

Alex wanders away feeling strangely invigorated, and impulsively decides on buying a drink from the vending machine, which stands just out of view from the chattering Wiccans. As he fiddles with the loose change in his pocket, curiosity gets the better of him. Glancing back around the corner to the table he has just left, Jasmine's distinctive voice can still be heard.

'It's hard not to notice, Penny, that you really like Alex. And it's also obvious the feeling from him is entirely mutual. When you are together, your auras radiate a light like I have never seen.'

With a flushed embarrassment, Penny coyly interjects, 'So do you think we're a match made in heaven then, with our planets in perfect alignment?'

Jasmine reaches out, placing her hand on Penny's. 'His path has already been chosen. It's all in his eyes... I see the darkness within him.'

'What do you mean?' demands a particularly agitated Penny. 'You keep going on about his bloody eyes, and I'm obviously missing something here. So what the hell is it you actually see when you look in them?'

Jasmine's compassion for her friend brings the one reply Penny never wanted to hear: 'I see his ruin..

Alex, having been back at Gabbitas Terrace for some time, hears the door lock rattle as Sam arrives home. On rushing across to the door, Alex holds the handle tight while jamming his shoulder firmly against it.

Sam struggles briefly with the handle. 'Come on, Alex, let me in. This is bloody juvenile.'

'Ha, ha, piss off,' laughs Alex, as Sam barges into the door with one last effort.

'Okay,' cedes Sam, 'I'll just take this bottle of vodka elsewhere.'

Here the front door opens immediately. 'Now, Samuel, let's not be too hasty–' as Alex leads Sam along the gloomy passageway by his upper arm. 'I'll go and get the glasses.'

While Alex is busy in the kitchen, Sam wanders into the perpetually cold living room and places his bottle next to a stack of old books with worn bindings piled up on the table. These tomes were of such an age, their pages barely kept together. And all the titles very peculiar: with Mysteriorum Libri Quinque, and Clavicula Solomonis just baffling to him.

Just as Sam takes his jacket off, Alex is once again back in the room with the glasses. 'There you go, Mr Bagwell,' says Alex, on quickly pouring the drinks and handing one to his friend.

As they both fall silent momentarily, enjoying their favourite tipple, the pile of books catches Sam's eye once more.

'God, Alex, these books here are in a right old state – what are they all about? And their names are a bit strange as well.'

'Oh, those,' Alex replies nonchalantly. 'Just some books that the reference library in the town was getting rid of.'

Sam smiles on shrugging his shoulders, and raises his glass to his friend. 'Oh well, good health.'

'So, Alex, have you seen any more of those new age chums of yours? And you don't honestly believe in all of that silly stuff, do you?'

Alex lowers his eyes to the floor after taking another sip from his glass. 'I believe in Penny.'

'Ah, so that's it,' laughs Sam, 'I knew there has to be something going on with one of them. So what have you been up to, you old devil? Spill the beans, I'm all ears.'

Alex sits down on the cracked old leather settee. 'Nothing's been going on, Sam. I really like Penny, and

I know she feels the same, but there is one huge sodding spanner in the works.'

Sam sits down next to Alex, taking a sip from his glass. 'Come on then, who is this spanner?'

'The spanner is Jasmine. She doesn't trust me, and to be honest I don't care for her. But she has an awful lot of influence over Penny, does High Priestess Delmont, too much.'

Sam sighs in consolation for his friend. 'So, what now? Where do you take it from here?'

Alex stares intently towards the pile of books on the table. 'I have an idea how to get Penny away from bloody Jasmine. Get her moving in different circles with me, so to speak.'

'You know that will be far easier said than done. You must know that, Alex.'

Picking at the fraying edges of his pullover cuff, Alex looks to Sam. 'When I see Penny next, in the squash courts, the canteen, or anywhere, I'm going to try and talk her round. It's getting to the point where all of my thoughts are just concentrated on her alone... Anyway, I'll have a quick sift through those old library books later. But in the meantime shall we finish this vodka?'

Sam holds his glass high in the air. 'Now you're talking my kind of language.'

The alarm clock calls its seven sharp beeps, but Alex is already awake. And the sun has been shining strongly through the threadbare curtains for well over two hours. As Sam moans and wriggles around slowly under his blankets in the bed opposite, he sits up and begins rubbing away at his dry and tired eyes.

'Bloody hell,' mocks Alex. 'The dead do rise.'

Sam combines a chuckle with a yawn and a stretch, as he reaches across to a small cabinet. And taking hold of his watch fastens it to his wrist. Looking across to Alex, who appears completely lost in his own thoughts, Sam utters, 'Whenever I stirred through the night, Alex, you always seemed to be awake. Still got a lot on your mind, eh?'

Alex swings his legs out of bed, slapping his feet to the floor. 'Oh, I'm fine. Surely I must have got at least forty winks in last night, so I'm feeling as fresh as a daisy in the morning dew.'

Sam climbs out of bed and begins to get dressed while looking on his friend with caution. 'Alex, I'm not being funny, but nobody lies awake all night when things are fine. And you don't look particularly fresh, or like a bloody daisy. So what's up, eh?'

Alex ties his shoelaces in a half-hearted spirit. 'It's Penny, I was thinking about meeting her again today. Just going over and over in my head what I want to say, and finding the right situation to say it.'

Sam smiles, jokingly responding with, 'Ah, love's young dream.'

'Fuck you!' snaps Alex. 'So what about your mythical girlfriend, who appears to keep your knackers in her purse?'

Sam quickly holds up his hands 'Hey, hey, steady on, Alex. Jesus, I was only joking with you.'

Alex shakes his head while abruptly directing his anger towards himself. 'Shit, I'm sorry, Sam. I just don't know what's happening to me. Just take no notice. And I didn't mean any of what I said about your other half either.'

Sam ruffles Alex's hair with his hand. 'No worries, it's all forgotten about; I just need to quickly pop out for a while anyhow.'

Alex stands up with his eyes glazed, asking Sam where he's going. Here Sam winks to Alex. 'Just popping out to meet the other half.' And as the front door closes, Alex slowly drops down onto the bed while holding his head in his hands.

Alex hurries along the transparent tunnelled entrance of Church Park leisure centre, with far too many troubles on his mind. He sees Jasmine, Penny and several others heading in the direction of the squash courts. And on quietly sneaking up behind Penny, Alex throws his arms around her. 'Argh! The Devil's coming.'

Penny bursts into a fit of giggles, while all of this is closely observed by Jasmine. 'Yes, the Devil,' she mutters.

Jasmine walks on unimpressed, leaving Alex and Penny alone for the very first time outside of the same squash court where their eyes first met. They beam with happiness, holding each other's hands. 'Are you going to join with our circle, Alex? We'll be able to do so much more together. I never thought I could be so happy.'

Alex kisses Penny on the cheek. 'Yes Penny, we'll have lots of time together; but just the two of us maybe, away from the coven.'

Penny pulls a puzzled expression. 'How do you mean, Alex, I don't understand where you're coming from?'

'Well,' blurts Alex excitedly, 'you know how this Wicca stuff is really just some worship of nature and the elements?'

Penny nods along. 'Yes, I follow you.'

'I've found some really ancient books,' says Alex gleefully, 'that teach real Magick. We can manipulate nature and the elements, all for our gain. And everything you've ever dreamed about, you'll be able to have.'

Penny takes a step back, horrified. 'Alex, these are the darkest of arts. Why would you even dream of turning your back to the light – what is your reason?'

'I have my reasons,' snaps Alex. 'And that's reason enough. Cross that abyss with me, Penny. Become a follower of the left hand path, and the secret knowledge that it hides.'

Penny's eyes slowly begin to fill up with tears. 'Please, Alex, come and join our circle. We've just been blessed with a chance to be happy; don't throw it all away.'

Alex finds a lump swelling in his throat. 'Come with me, Penny, leave Jasmine and the others behind. You don't need them; we can do so much more.'

Here Penny sobs bitterly. 'A heart of thorns; Jasmine sees just a heart of thorns when she looks into your eyes, Alex. She says your path can only bring ruin, and it's a route in all good conscience I just cannot take.'

Alex finds himself emotionally shattered. 'I need you,' he says.

Penny blinks repeatedly on wiping away her tears with an embroidered handkerchief. 'What you ask of me, Alex, I can't give. You want more, and though I'm sure you will find it, you can do so alone.'

Penny, now turning her back on Alex, begins to walk away. 'Will I see you tomorrow?' he shouts. And Penny gives no reply...

Alex's gaze is still firmly fixed at the window, as he becomes aware of a sudden and sharp nudging in his ribcage.

'Hey, Alex,' laughs Sam. 'Wake up, you've been daydreaming.'

Alex finds it difficult to answer with the welling lump in his throat. 'You got me thinking back to that summer in 1991 when I met Penny Goldman at Church

Park. I really liked her, Sam. All I ever wanted from her was to trust me; and I couldn't even do that.'

'Yeah, I remember,' says Sam, as he comforts Alex with a reassuring pat on the back. 'Don't worry, there'll always be another fish in the sea.'

Alex forces a smile. 'Yeah, I don't doubt it. But Penny was the only fish for me. I tried often, but could never find her again.'

Sam pours them another glass of vodka, and decides on bringing the subject back to earlier on in the evening. 'Alex, do you really think you should be reuniting with your old nemesis tomorrow, at a bare knuckle prize fight of all things? Imagine the sorts of characters who'll be turning up for that.'

Alex shakes his head. 'Now come on, Samuel, all arrangements were made and we shook on it. The only way you can get out of this now, is a note from Matron. Do you have a note from Matron, Sam?'

Sam stands up, agitated. 'I wish I had a bloody Matron to tell you to piss off. But seeing as I don't, I'm just going to piss off for a piss instead.'

Alex tops up both drinks with the last few remaining drops from the bottle as Sam comes back into the room. Sam yawns and stretches on flopping down into the comfy chair. 'This vodka has rendered me close to absolute annihilation,' he says to Alex. Who himself at this point begins to struggle with the simple action of focusing his eyes on his friend.

'Sam, I pulled out the sofa bed for you earlier, as I had an idea, well, a very good idea, that we'd end up oblivious. My alarm's set for six o'clock in the morning, so if we turn in now we'll get seven hours' snooze with any luck. Now all that's left for me is to endure the epic voyage of manoeuvring myself from this spot and up to my bed.'

Alex shuffles himself to the door as Sam yawns. 'Sounds good to me, Alex, I'm ready for a snooze. Switch the lights off on your way out as well please; night, night.'

Sam opens his laboured eyes, having been disturbed by the shrieks from a passing flock of seagulls. And the door opens slightly as Alex peeps through the crack. 'Ah, good, Sam, you're awake.'

Sam draws down his covers and sits up. 'What time is it, Alex?'

'It's twenty past six, Sam. I was just about to wake you up. Do you want some toast and a cup of tea? I'm having some.'

Sam sits up and begins pulling on his denim jeans. 'Oh, yes please. Something to help soak up all of that vodka would be ideal.'

Alex claps his hands together firmly. 'Right, I'll just be two shakes, Mr Bagwell.'

By the time Alex appears back in the sitting room, Sam is already folding away his blankets. 'There you go, Squire,' chirps Alex.

'Well, thank you kindly, Governor,' replies Sam as he sits down, hungrily munching away on his toast, and blowing on his hot tea.

Alex sits down opposite and begins to put on his shoes. 'Right, Sam, when you get that down you we'll have a slow walk across the back fields. With the fisticuffs being arranged for eight, we should get there in plenty of time.'

'I'll go for the walk,' Sam carries on, 'but I've got no interest whatsoever in being a spectator to a human cockfight.'

Alex begins pulling on his black leather jacket. 'Oh, fuss, fuss, fuss; come on, Sam.'

Sam stands up as Alex passes him his beige raincoat. 'Okay Alex, let's get this bloody thing over and done with. And I was thinking that if I leave here around tea time, I'll get home just in time to sort things out for work tomorrow.'

Alex nods to his friend. 'Yep, sounds like a plan to me, old bean. Right, where's my bloody keys gone?' On scanning the room, Alex spots them on his bookcase. 'Ah, there they are. You go out first, Sam, while I set the burglar alarm. I've never had a break in before, but who knows what the future brings.'

Sam steps out of the door, smiling. 'Peace of mind, Alex, it's all worth it for the peace of mind.'

Sam has been walking forever, or at least this is what his aching legs are telling him. 'Bloody hell, Alex, how far now? I can get out of breath just jogging my memory these days.'

'Not far now, Sam,' laughs Alex. 'Well, can you see that stone wall in the distance?'

'Yes, I see it. But if that's the direction we are heading in, where's the gate?'

Alex abruptly stops in his tracks. 'There is no gate. We climb over it. That's the one pitfall in us taking this shortcut. Did I not tell you, Sam?'

'No, Alex, you pissing well didn't tell me. But we've walked too far now to turn back. So when we get to the wall, you are helping me over it, agreed?'

Alex looks ahead of him as he pats Sam on the back. 'Agreed.'

This grey stone wall must be the best part of eight feet in height, as with Alex's help, Sam struggles over the top and drops to the grass verge of the road. Very shortly afterwards, Alex drops from the wall as Sam dusts himself down while looking around. 'Well, this seems to be the arse end of nowhere.'

'Yeah, Sam, it's really quiet along this stretch of road. Just used by farmers mainly. And it looks like the birds can't even muster enough interest to fly around here.' They both scan the meadows and lanes in the distance, until Alex spots a broken down car not so far away.

Its red bonnet is propped up, and a woman beneath it is tinkering with the engine. 'Hey Sam, do you remember how I was talking about Penny Goldman yesterday?'

'Yes, Alex, I recall that I set you off in that train of thought. Why do you mention her?'

Alex squints his eyes tightly while peering at the car. 'I'm bloody certain that's Penny over there.'

'Penny!' shouts Alex, waving his arms above his head. And here a short haired and slight woman in a blue blazer appears from underneath the bonnet, rubbing around her oily hands with an old length of cloth.

'My word, Alexander Villiers.' Penny gasps with surprise. 'I never thought I'd bump into you again. What brings you along to this neck of the woods?'

Alex nods with a smile. 'I was just about to ask you the same thing. Oh, and by the way, this is Sam, a good friend from the old days.'

Penny takes a step forward. 'Delighted to meet you, Sam, how do you do?'

'I'm very well, Penny, thanks, and how are you?'

Penny turns around, gesturing with her thumb. 'Oh, I'm fine. But this disaster on wheels has fallen out with its fan belt again. I hadn't long been on the phone to the roadside recovery when I heard Alex calling my name.'

Alex stands with his arms folded in a pleasantly comfortable manner. 'It's funny that we've bumped into you, Penny. I was thinking about you only yesterday.'

The screeching of tyres brings this old rusted car to a halt. 'Eh Alex, I thought that was you,' comes a gruff voice through a slack mouth of dirty and broken teeth.

And here, neither Alex nor Sam appear totally at ease with this enormous and slovenly sight now accosting them.

'Ah, Missy Mullins,' says Alex, giving his very best efforts at being warm and cordial. 'It's quite strange seeing you again after all of this time.'

Missy scrunches up her face: a complexion that Alex had likened to grainy leather. 'What do you mean, strange?'

Alex chuckles nervously. 'Oh come on, Missy, let's not get off on the wrong foot again.' And here Sam and Penny look at each other uncomfortably while taking a slight step back.

'I'll put my wrong foot right up your arse if you fucking start with me, Alex,' she bellows.

Alex stands up on his tiptoes in a poor attempt to look his former tormentor in the eye. 'Yes, Missy, I'm certain you could. But in the meantime, let me introduce you to my friends–' as Alex waves them both over. 'Sam and Penny, this is Missy.'

Here both Sam and Penny nod nervously in the direction of this frightening woman.

'Alright?' barks Missy.

Penny nods again without any eye contact being made. 'I'm fine.'

Missy glares at her. 'Hey Alex, is this cunt trying to be fucking funny, eh?'

And before Alex gets a chance to respond, a convoy of cars begin passing them in succession down the lane. As they watch, Penny looks about her with a puzzled expression. 'I wonder where all of those cars are going.'

Sam and Alex simultaneously clear their throats, as Missy shouts out, 'Going to the frigging fight, man, you stupid little bitch.' And turning to Alex, Missy barks, 'Is this arsehole thick, or just taking the piss, eh?'

Penny looks to the ground anxiously, and placing her hands into her blazer pockets takes several steps backwards. 'I'm sorry, Missy, but I've no intention of offending you.'

'Don't Missy me, you stupid posh cunt. I'll slit your fucking throat!'

Penny fumbles around in her pocket, taking out her mobile phone. 'Alex, I'm just going to wait in the car now as the breakdown van should be here soon, and I have a couple of calls to make, okay?' Penny nods to Alex as she hurriedly begins making her way back to the car.

On climbing inside, she immediately locks all of the doors, and with her hands shaking, dials 999 on her phone. 'Hello, police?' she enquires timidly. 'Yes, I'm in a spot of bother. The thing is I'm waiting for a breakdown van to come along and assist me. But there's also an awful woman here; her behaviour is excessively threatening and abusive. I'm not one to waste police time whatever the circumstance, but could you send an officer out until the recovery van arrives, please? I just don't feel safe.' Penny listens on intently. 'I'm on a road I think is called Deeks Lane, and it looks to be surrounded by farmland.' Falling silent again for several moments, she gasps, 'Oh, thank you. Ten minutes? Great, see you then.'

On the road, Alex is livid with Missy. 'Hey! Have you got to fucking talk to my friend like that, you arsehole?'

Missy points to Penny's car, bellowing, 'She was taking the piss, man! So are we going to this fucking fight or not? I just want to see someone getting killed.'

Sam laughs in disbelief at what he hears. 'Bloody hell, Missy, you don't pull any punches.'

'Eh, what?' she asks indignantly, while adjusting the strap of her mud splashed shoulder bag. 'Come on then, what are you two fuckwits waiting for! Is it Christmas?'

'Missy, Missy' says Alex. 'I saw this prize fight last night, and believe me you will end up sorely disappointed because no one gets killed: a very poor effort overall.'

'How could you see the fucking fight when it hasn't even happened yet, Villiers?' scoffs Missy in a cynical tone. 'Fucking shit for brains.'

'Au contraire,' replies Alex, brimming with confidence. 'You see, I participated in a spot of astrological path working last night, Missy. A meditation if you like; with my trusty Thoth Tarot deck. And that's how I became a party to a preview of this much anticipated brawl.'

Missy glares furiously in the direction of Sam. 'Is this daft cunt Villiers for fucking real?'

Sam, feeling very out of sorts in a situation such as this, utters, 'Hey, I don't know what Alex means, honestly I don't.'

'That's correct,' Alex concurs. 'I did this when all alone. Sam had nothing to do with it.'

An enraged Missy lunges forward, making a grab for Alex, who then just barely manages to evade her grasp. 'Don't wind me up, Villiers, or I'll give you a good fucking kicking.'

'You can't ever compete with me, Missy, so don't even think about it,' growls Alex.

Missy throws her head back, letting out a hideous cackle. 'Ha! I brayed the shit out of you at school. And there's no way a fucking lanky jellyfish like you could do anything about it now.'

'But I did do something about it,' spits Alex as his agitation heightens. 'And the joy of it all is that with you being such a fucking moron, you were too thick to ever realise.'

'How! Eh? How did you get me? It's bullshit!' screams Missy.

'Well,' says Alex, now calming in his temperament. 'Where shall I begin? Some years back at Church Park leisure centre, I met a lovely White Witch called Penny; who now sits in that car just over there, you see?'

Missy stands and looks across to Penny, while folding her arms and tutting incredulously.

'Ah, never mind the tuts, Missy,' continues Alex. 'And Penny – who I brought here by the way, although she has no knowledge of it yet – bless her. She unwittingly introduced me to a world I'd never have imagined before. I found a chance to hurt you, Missy, without ever needing to lay a finger on your pig ugly form.'

Missy looks Alex up and down in absolute disgust. 'What the fuck are you on about, Villiers?'

'The Occult, dipshit, or call it whatever, you brain dead bastard!' shouts Alex, while turning almost purple in his fury. 'I might have lost Penny, but I still got you back good and proper, Missy. I fucking well got you!'

Penny sits nervously but gratefully locked inside her car, while watching these antagonistic events unfolding before her. And nervously fidgets while counting the seconds until either the recovery van or the police themselves arrive.

Missy's long scraggily hair flies in all directions as she screams, 'You got me? How the fuck did you get me? I'm sick of you talking shit.'

Here Sam steps forward, trying his best to smooth things over and diffuse the situation. 'Come on, let's all just calm things down somehow, eh?' And here he's greeted by a glare from both that lets him know beyond doubt this certainly isn't the time to be placatory.

'Now,' says Alex, 'Let me think. Just how the hell did I get you? Oh yes, it was such a shame about your husband, wasn't it?'

Missy curtly points a finger firmly into Alex's face. 'Leave George out of this, you little cunt. He's got nothing to do with anything.'

Alex chuckles in a sarcastic tone, 'Oh Missy, I'm afraid that George is at the very heart of the matter. While chopping meat at the butcher's shop, I heard he had a little accident, severing an artery. And by all accounts, the note he'd received with this order insisted that the meat be cut there and then.'

Missy pulls a gruesome expression while rolling her eyes. 'Yeah, the police showed me the note. It was covered in stupid fucking shapes and squiggles. Just like the ones some daft cunt had put inside the twins' first birthday card, so!'

'And where are those twins now?' gloats Alex.

'In a bastard mental hospital!' yells Missy, clutching tightly onto her shoulder bag strap. 'No doubt you'll know that already, Villiers, with your stupid ghost magic, or whatever it is. So why fucking ask?'

'I was asking, Missy, as I must admit I've waited such a long time that I'm really looking forward to this. To inform you I'm the architect of your ill fortune. Those stupid shapes and squiggles are symbols used in Enochian Magick, to evoke demons. And even that noble dark art of Thorn Canker came in particularly useful.'

Missy, shaking her head manically, cries, 'So what are you fucking saying?'

Alex steps in close to Missy's face. 'I'm fucking saying I did lose Penny, but gained a power to destroy your family for what you did to me. So, there you go, Missy, I'm to blame for what happened to George and those twins. Favour returned!' And here Alex spits directly into Missy's furious face.

Wiping the spit away, Missy pushes Alex hard in the chest as he loses his balance, falling backwards. 'Right, I'll slit your fucking throat, Villiers.'

Sam lunges forward as Missy pulls a long filleting knife from her shoulder bag. 'Oh, come on,' pleads Sam. 'There really is just no need for this.'

Missy lets out a hideous screech while swinging the blade, and slashing Sam across the throat as he clutches tightly around his collar with a look of abject terror.

He drops to his knees as through the windscreen of the car in the distance, Penny's horrified screams are muted. She bounces up and down in her seat, frantically thumping the car's horn with the heel of her hand in desperate panic.

The moment Sam drops to the floor, Alex gets to his feet to find this tragedy before him. He looks to his old nemesis while kneeling over his wounded friend. 'You stupid bastard, Missy, what have you done?' Sam rolls around gasping for air, while Alex tries desperately to stem the profuse bleeding. 'Come on, Sam, stay with me. I'll get an ambulance, okay.'

Sam's pallor drains away as Alex cradles his friend's head, and turning his vengeful scowl to Missy. 'It should have been me, you stupid bitch! Not Sam. Do you hear?'

'It's going to be you,' replies Missy with an astonishing calmness, as Alex turns his attentions back to his dying friend. And swinging her arm again with a ferocious cry, she jams the knife so forcefully into the side of Alex's head, the weapon's blade snaps clean on impact.

He slumps down over Sam, and rolls onto his back. Here Missy becomes hypnotised by the sight of her victim's eyes being flushed with the blackest blood. He stares deeply into her gaze, and curses, 'Like a raven on a rotting gibbet, cawing at an eyeless head, flesh be torn and bones ripped bare, tearing 'til your soul be shred.'

A police siren is heard faintly in the distance as Penny hides her face from the trauma. And Missy stands frozen still as Alex gasps a heavy breath on closing his eyes for the final time. He lies on the road motionless, and as always, with his best friend Sam at his side...

Missy's manic screams in the night melt into the other wailing cries heard from neighbouring cells of the Halstead Hill mental institution. 'I can't take it anymore,' she sobs hysterically, pulling at her hair. 'I need to fucking sleep! Somebody help me.'

Suddenly every noise about her stops, save for an unusual sound of dripping. Missy peers down to the left hand side of the bed, seeing a slow trickle of blood meandering across the floor towards her. But the more Missy scrutinises this, the more sensible she now becomes to movement and the faintest whisper of a voice in the far corner of the shadowy room. 'I'm here, Missy, to help you.'

In her vigilance, Missy glances to this now inhabited corner, only to scream and sob once again. Missy's husband George is slumped there; his emaciated skin a putrefying grey. A blood drenched butcher's apron drips steadily as the gaping wound of his maggot eaten arm still weeps: these decomposing features being the very depths of torment.

Through a ravaged and soulless voice, George beckons to Missy. 'I'll take you with me, my love. The great beast Baphomet himself awaits you, his bride. He commands the anointing of his Whore of Babylon, my kindest; and in his mighty wisdom has chosen you!' George begins to howl manically on levitating upwards with his arms outstretched.

'Christ! Help me!' screams Missy. 'Leave me alone. I can't fucking take anymore...'

Missy is discovered the next morning by a nurse. She is sitting bolt upright; her eyes forced wide in dread. Bound in that exact same position her defeated spirit abandoned only hours before. And there she's carted away to the silence of a mortuary; literally scared to death.

Solomon's Quay

These abrasions on his knuckles are as raw as they were yesterday, and just as stinging sore. He grimaces while dabbing these readily endured wounds with a salt watered cloth. A white powder hastily ingested through a makeshift straw sets his teeth grinding hard. On surveying the populace before him, paranoia strikes on noticing a face he's never come across before. All in all, it's probably quite a bad time to test out this particularly potent cocaine; but now is still assumed to be as good a time as any.

The gathering observe this awkward man trying his very best to compose himself in front of them. And he may well court accusations of characteristic imperfections – but in their eyes, Reverend Donald Jaggers, looking out from his pulpit, is an always comforting sight.

Following a stirring rendition of The Lord Is Thy Shepherd, Don hands a golden tin plate to the nearest of his 'flock', to be passed about for all donations obligingly given. As it weaves its way around the parishioners, he witnesses this unrecognised patron allowing the plate to pass him by. Don isn't prepared to stand for any of this nonsense, and promptly decides on confronting this 'unrepentant little shit' when the service draws to a close.

As this pious congregation head towards the exit of Sentinel's Church, Don makes a beeline towards a tubby man in purple dungarees and a cloth cap. On confronting this fellow – who on being taken unawares hastily introduces himself as Jackie Trattles – Don immediately cuts to the chase. 'You're a cheeky bastard, aren't you? Never showing your face in here before, and you didn't even have the decency to put a single pissing penny onto the collection plate. Could you explain to me what that's all about?'

Jackie, at first overwhelmed by a cursing vicar with weeping knuckles, apologises profusely. 'I'm sorry, Reverend, and I'm by no means a devout man, and never wished to cause offence, but I desperately seek the guidance from a man of the cloth.'

Don, grinding his teeth, stares at Jackie through bloodshot eyes. 'So why have you never sat in this house of our Lord before today, then? Have you taken a liking to vicars and fonts all of a sudden?'

Feeling somewhat intimidated, Jackie clears his throat to begin his explanation. 'Well I've just recently moved into one of the late Victorian houses along Solomon's Quay.'

'I see,' replies the Reverend dismissively. 'I'd like to be of some assistance, but I'm currently preoccupied at the moment arranging a twelfth night Christmas party for the children of The Gingerbread Club. So for the time being at least, this must remain my priority.'

And without another word spoken by either man, Jackie wanders away despondently...

With Sentinel's now thankfully empty after this dragging service, Don hurries off through the archaic ruins of the snow sprinkled churchyard and across the frost hardened playing fields of Templar's Primary School, muttering aloud how beneficial several bottles of brown ale will be at this particular time. But on looking towards one of the tinsel decorated classrooms, he notices odd shadowy movements and distant clattering sounds. Don, knowing the kids are still on their Christmas holidays, heads over towards the suspicious activity, and manages to squeeze through a gap in the unusually loose fire escape door.

Crawling on all fours, he approaches the room where the Gingerbread twelfth night party is to be held. Moving eye level to a window, he peers through, seeing three flailing youths ripping away the decorations and baubles from a tree as it falls to the floor. Don, being so furious at witnessing this act of wanton destruction, grinds his teeth until his energy and anger explode. Kicking open the unlatched corridor window, he forces it wider still with his foot. And now suddenly confronts these destructive young men, in this already locked classroom.

'Hello lads, I see you've turned over the tuck shop, before your fun began in here,' says Don as he scrutinizes the damage caused by these vandals. 'It's a bit fucking spiteful doing this to the little kids, isn't it? What do you three think you're playing at?'

The most confident of this rough and scruffy gang spits phlegm onto the floor, just missing Don's polished shoe. 'If you don't want knocking out, you'd do well to fuck off, Mister Vicar. And try minding your own business in future. It wouldn't take much effort for us to punch some poncy twat like you into a coma.'

Don takes several measured steps backwards, lifting both open palms shoulder high. 'Message understood loud and clear, lads. I don't want any more trouble here.'

Grabbing a chair, Don swings with both arms, crashing the wooden seat into the face of the closest offender. While the other two rush to escape, he grabs one hanging halfway out of the window by the waistband, kicking him full force in the groin. And the third intruder, who'd so bravely issued the threat, now pleads frantically as Don drags him close by the collars, and head-butts this whimpering lad in the mouth with such ferocity that his teeth split out through his bottom lip. On pulling off his steel buckled leather belt, this livid holy-man whips the lads senseless, until they somehow manage to escape through any exit with their lives intact.

Breathless from his rage and sudden flurry of effort, Don calmly begins tidying up the room. Applying his most concentrated effort, he carefully drapes all ruined decorations back around this damaged tree. On sweeping up the broken glass and mopping away the drizzles of blood, he leaves a note informing the school caretaker about this disturbance. And finally he heads off towards the Ark & Amulet pub for his brown ale, and a hopefully less eventful evening...

A 'wake and bake' now begins Don's day: with a cannabis pipe being the miracle cure for all maladies. And on brewing some decaffeinated coffee, the hot drink requires an added extra: this being a good old fashioned hair of the dog. But Don suddenly grimaces on realising his malt whisky bottle is empty. This being one of several 'tonics' he keeps as emergency rations – and a voyage into the bleak outdoors to bolster supplies is now inevitable.

Having made every effort possible to keep warm, on stepping outside, he still finds shivering remarkably easy. With his sight partially blurring from cannabis blindness, Don is just about able to make out a figure approaching. On rubbing his reddened eyes, Don finally focuses on the frozen features of Jackie Trattles.

It's hard not to notice that Jackie looks like he hasn't slept for a month; and sporting cuts and bruises that any game scrappers could be proud of. So Don decides upon engaging this weary fellow. 'Bloody hell, who's been roughing you up then?'

Jackie rubs one of his more painful wounds. 'I'm not sure who did this to me' comes the reply.

Appearing slightly bemused, Don laughs. 'You need to be a bit more careful around here, Jackie, especially with being a new face. As some twats down at Babel's Bay happily take advantage of a wandering stranger like yourself, and give them a thumping. And the same story goes along Solomon's Quay.'

Here Jackie's lower lip quivers uncontrollably. 'When I was being attacked I was alone in the house, and couldn't see anyone while this was happening.'

Don, on having no idea what to make of it all, hasn't a clue how to respond. But this chap certainly appears earnest in what he believes. 'How about you come across to the vicarage around eight, Jackie? We'll discuss this further later tonight, eh?'

An almost teary Jackie exhales heavily in gratitude and relief, confirming he'll certainly be there.

On remembering the date being December 31st, Don hastily acquires several large bottles of spirits from Mr Conrad Singh's Mini Market; and heads off to meet with the church council regarding the kids' party. There bringing this manic Yuletide lark to a much welcomed close.

While snorting two lines of 'livener' on his study desk, Don's teeth begin to grind hard again. And his mind wanders back to the previous evening's antics in the Ark & Amulet pub. Where the always steroid fuelled local gangsters Tommy Frame and Pat Fennec have been goading him on a consistent basis, blatantly spoiling for a fight. And in Don's best efforts to dispel his edgy symptom, he smokes a cannabis pipe. But this only facilitates a thirst for a large glass of one of his many favourite tipples...

Don revives himself with a start from some kind of drug bubble he has been trapped inside for the past several hours. He makes a flustered and apologetic phone call to an unimpressed parish councillor, making his excuses for missing the meeting. And promises he will collect a copy of the minutes from the secretary first thing tomorrow. As the day has virtually passed Don by, he decides to have a couple of drinks down at the pub, and be back in time for Jackie's visit in a matter of hours.

The Ark & Amulet is still busy with these early doors revellers this New Year's Eve, as Don squeezes his way to the bar for his usual. On looking about for familiar faces, he finds it hard not to notice that Tommy and Pat are already in residence. As Don quietly waits for his drink, Tommy quickly approaches him and blindsides the priest with a hard elbow in the ribs. Don, flinching from this assault by his goading nemesis, gets this incident nipped in the bud.

'Hey! Just fuck off back to your brain damage club where you belong, Tommy. You strutting prick. I've got some parish business later on, and would prefer to be left alone, thanks.'

Following another sharp elbow into Don's ribs, this strutting prick needles his target further. 'Oh, I hear you're organising some kids' party soon, Jaggers. So it is true that vicars prefer them young. You must be chomping at the bit to get started touching them up in the vestry.'

With things now taken to this point of no return by his too confident foe, Don removes his white collar. 'Right, that's the finish, Tommy, you arsehole. It's clearly obvious that violence is all you and your inbred boyfriend Fennec ever crave. And in this regard, you have both just hit the fucking jackpot, because we're going to sort this out properly, in the car park.'

As Don steps outside, taking off his black jacket, he yanks a length of steel drain piping from the pub wall and swings it wildly, as if taking a scythe to overgrown grass. As the bellowing Fennec bursts out through the swinging doors, this heavy pipe smashes into both knee caps, dropping him into a crippled heap. And now hot in pursuit is the more dangerous antagonist Frame, who struts outside menacingly while stepping over his curled up cohort.

Don, dropping the pipe, takes several steps backwards across the rough icy gravel and circles his sneering foe. 'This is what you've wanted, Tommy, a scrap with the vicar. And now it's just you and me... Let's go.'

Here some congregating voyeurs are compelled to watch while both bloodthirsty combatants absorb several horrifying bare knuckled exchanges. And with each man's fortunes fluctuating violently, Don, though bloodied and beaten, destroys his victim's defences with a sharp right hook that floors him. The crowd shriek loudly on realising this brawler's arm has scraped the gravelled surface so severely that his skin has rolled up the now raw limb like a sleeve. And here Don witnesses his suddenly ruined adversary weeping bitterly in despair.

'Have you had enough, big man?' shouts Don, while spitting away the blood that drips from his mouth.

Choking back hard on his tears, Tommy cries out, 'Fuck off, Jaggers, you bastard. Fucking leave me alone!'

Don glares murderously at the helpless hard man. 'Do you know what? People like you, Tommy, can never have enough.' And there kicks out forcefully with the bridge of his foot, splitting wide the already shattered nose of his vulnerable target as the bystanders quickly intervene. Demanding the fight to be over with; and 'enough is enough'...

When Don finally arrives at the gothic vicarage, Jackie is already waiting. It's nowhere near 8 o'clock, so this bloodied clergyman is under no illusions that things must really need addressing in the mind of his visitor. And greeting one another by the icicle draped iron gate, Don directs Jackie along the barely visible pathway and onwards into the house.

Don pours himself a glass of Sloe Gin, and, taking the liberty, does likewise for his visitor and sits down opposite Jackie in their large leather chairs.

'I'm sorry about the swollen hands and limp, Jackie. But I think I might have fractured some bones in my foot on some arsehole's face. Anyway, enough about me; how are your scratches and scrapes healing?'

Jackie sits slightly bewildered. 'To be honest, Don, I was just about to enquire exactly the same of you.' And here Don describes in much detail his physical encounter from earlier that evening.

Jackie comments on how strange it is for a man of the cloth to possess such a temperament that could possibly be deemed unsuitable for a clergyman. On sitting back in his chair, Don admits that others have broached this subject before. And have all failed in producing valid explanations while portraying the psychoanalyst.

'We're all contrary characters if we delve deep enough,' says Don to his curious companion, 'all perfectly capable of committing deeds both good and evil. And that applies to everyone, including me.'

Jackie, hanging on every word, comments, 'I assumed it was some kind of unwritten rule that the clergy were quiet, unassuming men.'

This smiling reverend looks innocently to his inquisitor. 'My only reply to that, Jackie, is along with hearts and bones, rules will always get broken.'

Don then reaches across a polished table, offering Jackie a cannabis pipe, which he gratefully declines... On blowing upwards a fresh jet of dense smoke, Don tells Jackie, 'I've stooped to violence when all else has failed. But no man stands taller than he who stoops to help a child; including those little monkeys in The Gingerbread Club. Whose twelfth night party is signed and sealed for next week.'

And being almost too carried away by this honest display of emotion and affection towards the children, Don clears his throat. 'So, Jackie, let's get back to business. From the beginning, what exactly happened to you, and when did it all start?'

'Well,' says Jackie, 'when I first moved into 5 Solomon's Quay, there were a lot of noises around me, in whichever room I went. On not wanting to make anything more of it at this point, I put it down to creaks in the floorboards or rusted pipes in the old heating system. But on retiring to bed, I began feeling the tapping of a finger on my shoulder, which immediately stopped when pulling down my blankets to sit upright.'

And here Don furrows his brow, deep in concentration, while Jackie continues. 'Then came the gentle pulling on odd strands of my hair, which has always been quite coarse, like hay; and as the evenings rolled on, clumps were yanked at so hard my head lifted off the pillow. And now I'm awoken by an actual physical assault; but nobody is ever there.'

Jackie pauses for composure while Don empties a small bag of cocaine onto the table. On snorting two small lines, it isn't long before his teeth are grinding and he rests back into his chair. With an edgy look in his eye, he replies to his concerned acquaintance, 'Jackie, when I became the parish reverend some fifteen years ago, I was expected to do my homework on the area; which covered Solomon's Quay to the boundaries of Babel's Bay.'

And here Jackie squirms uneasily in his chair with the uncertainty of what may come.

'In 1843,' explains Don, 'two young men named Kingsley Jackson and Sebastian Pym lived at number 5 in that particular street. Both keen students of the dark arts, and apparently much admired in the community: particularly generous by all accounts. But it was only when both were discovered dead inside the property that their occult diaries surfaced, and were nothing short of an unsettling read.'

Don, stopping for a moment, swallows another gulp from his glass as Jackie likens to do the very same. With the drinks being topped up, Don continues divulging all he knows on these scholars of the esoteric doctrines.

'According to those diaries, young Kingsley and Sebastian summoned a demon named Choronzon, after realising themselves to be suddenly out of their depth. Apparently, a previously manifested entity began demanding fresh blood, so the lads decided they had no other choice but to evoke, what they presumed, an all commanding force to banish it. So when these frightened magicians called on Choronzon, they unleashed this so called Lord of Darkness into their world...'

Both men sit silent for several minutes as the only noises to be heard are the grinding of Don's teeth and the ticking of a clock. To lighten the darker mood somewhat, Don begins to quip, 'As you know, Jackie, I don't mind taking off my collar to give some of the local scum a good beating. But I'm not really sure how I'd fare in a scrap with a demon so notoriously vicious, that other entities presumably shit their pants at the mere mention of its name.'

Suddenly feeling so overcome by the Sloe Gin consumed over these last several hours, Jackie listens on contentedly while the neighbouring church clock begins its twelve chimes. Taking both inebriated companions quietly into the year 1989. On shaking hands and exchanging the usual seasonal wishes, Don assures his well-oiled friend that he'll visit his home tomorrow morning. There deciding what needs doing next to assure the wellbeing of his preoccupied visitor. Jackie again shakes hands with his welcoming host, thanking him for his time, and bids him farewell...

On shutting firm the front door of number 5, Jackie trembles, unsure whether it's the cold, or this horribly unsettling situation that finds him chilled to the bone. As he hurriedly flicks the switch to illuminate this gloomy passageway, the bulb fails. And there Jackie's panic stricken thoughts dwell on any scenario possible. 'Are there really supernatural beings that can ravage the souls of other entities? Are Kingsley and Sebastian lurking somewhere in these shadows? How many ghosts can haunt a bloody house, for fuck's sake?' And deciding it better not to get undressed, Jackie curls up on the settee while using his oversized Parka coat as a blanket.

A tapping finger at the bottom of this coat slowly moves its way up Jackie's shivering body until it reaches his shoulder. As he gasps in dread, there is that peculiar sensation of his hair being disturbed. His head then slowly warms with a mild vibration, before a violent quivering induces a skull imploding pressure. Jackie writhes and convulses in agony. 'Bloody get off! Don't hurt me!' he pleads in desperation, while his frantic cries echo about the house. And on covering his head with the fur-trimmed hood of his coat for protection, he cries hopelessly in the blackest night.

It has now just gone 6 o'clock on this bitter morning as Jackie realises he hasn't slept a wink. Upstairs a succession of room rattling thuds then begin, directly from the still vacant quarters above him; but now accompanied by a muffled shrieking. And despite Jackie's terror, the one single shred of hope spurring him is that Don Jaggers will keep to his word. And hopefully, somehow, remedy this unendurable situation...

A nip of whisky is poured into this cup of coffee as Don sits fully dressed and alert for such an early hour. He reaches across to a drawer, pulling out a shining crucifix. And pondering on this image of his faith for several seconds, he's about to put it into his jacket pocket, but stops for a moment. Musing on every occasion where the odds were stacked firmly against him in his 45 years. Remembering whatever the fight or cause, he always stood alone. Taking off his white collar, he places it, along with the cross, back into the drawer. And draining his alcohol-laced beverage, he picks up his keys before slamming the creaking door behind him...

Jackie opens the front door to an icy breeze, and looking along Solomon's Quay there is not a person in sight. On despondently stepping back inside, he leaves the door ajar as there is now a distinctly unpleasant odour drifting downstairs. On again sensing some agitation of his hair, a sudden force pushes his face slowly towards the protruding hooks of the wall mounted coat rack.

'No! You bloody bastard!' he cries, 'You're not doing this to me anymore!'

Holding his outstretched hands firm against the wall, he struggles frantically as his resistance begins to falter. Now having had all he can stomach of these attacks, Jackie's long dormant anger explodes. With a newfound conviction, he pushes himself clear of danger – only to be hurled across the floor by this unseen terror, as his head smashes into the splintering shards of the high skirting board.

The door at number 5 almost flies off its rusted hinges as Don bursts inside, finding a barely conscious Jackie with his forehead almost shredded.

'Christ, what's happened here, Jackie?'

While this silence is broken only by a whistling of wind, Don hears footsteps bounding up the staircase before him; yet nothing appears there. On quickly giving chase, he races up every step to the landing. And looking towards a dilapidated room, he becomes all too sensible to these dangers now accosting him. On stepping apprehensively into this doorway, the room is slowly engulfed with an eerie grey fog.

Taking off his jacket, he drops it down onto these creaking floorboards as they quickly begin to rattle.

'Right, you little fucker!' he shouts. 'Whatever you are, and wherever you're from, you don't belong here... And I'm telling you now there's only one of us can win.

But guess what? It's not going to be you... Do you hear me?'

Stepping into the centre of this room, Don is immediately incapacitated by a musky odour so abhorrent he vomits violently. On his attempts to recuperate and calm his racing breaths, the grey fog thickens about him as he's drawn down onto his knee. This mist constrictively swirls about his middle body, causing an excruciating pain. 'Argh, God... Jesus Christ. Help me,' he gasps. Imploring the good Lord to save him: to take him from the Devil's house.

Lying sideways in agony, Don sees two shimmering white shadows struggling through this eerie mist towards him. And he hears the urgent echoing cries of two young men: 'Don, call upon the keepers of the watchtowers', comes the faint, reverberating plea. 'This is your only salvation.'

As the thick fog swallows the two, Don curls tightly into a ball. Gasping out as he begins to drift in and out of his consciousness, he whispers, 'Keepers... Watchtowers... I call on you.' And suddenly these shadowy apparitions manifest dominantly through an explosion of sparkling light. Now channelling their energies through him, Don involuntarily summons the celestial forces of Raphael, Gabriel, Michael and Uriel.

After too many moments of silent dread, Don shrieks out in horror at the sudden and hellish emergence of a writhing serpent at his twitching feet. Without warning he's quickly shackled by the demon, as some mucus spewing membranes facilitate its rapid coiling up around him with each contraction of its visible intestines. As a slimy blackened tongue inches towards the reverend's gulping mouth, he's sickened by the inescapable aroma of rotting flesh.

On resigning to this battle being lost, Don is suddenly struck from the north face of the room by some heavenly bolt of blue light, hurling him to the south corner, where he's struck again. As he's flung helplessly to both east and west points, these angelic lights strike at him. Every flash aimed piercing the essence of this demonic force that binds him.

As a warm sparkling glow begins coursing its way around his body with a mild static surge, Don intuitively realises his soul is now armoured and impenetrable to any further malevolent attacks. 'Fuck off!' he shouts contemptibly, while enduring a final hideous screech from this eyeless aberration. Before it finally releases him; rapidly retreating back into the mists and stench of its own realm.

While this oppressive climate quickly evaporates, making way for a bright and crisply aired atmosphere, Don falls helplessly to the floor – paralysed in a shaken disbelief.

Several minutes later, in the bathroom, splashes of ice cold water are no longer a shock to the system for Reverend Donald Jaggers. And having eventually reached the bottom of the stairs, he finds Jackie Trattles is barely lucid. While trying to keep his own legs from buckling, Don pulls his friend upright by the arm. 'Come on, Jackie, you've just missed all the fun.'

Here Jackie, still visibly shaken, asks what happened upstairs. Don smiles. 'I've just met the old tenants: a helpful couple of lads I thought. As well as four flashy types we can only hope will hang around.'

Jackie, carefully picking wooden splinters from his forehead, enquires if his anonymous tormentor is gone. Don ruffles Jackie's hair like a kid's. 'There'll be no funny business going on tonight, Jackie. And you can take it from me,' he assures him.

Now overcome and wiping away tears of relief, he asks Don, 'How can I ever begin, in any way possible, to repay you for what you have just done for me?'

The only response from the grinning reverend being, 'It's funny you should ask that. I was just thinking that a fifty pence coin on the collection plate, once or twice a week, could be a very good place to start...'